A word from the author.
I am just your average Joe. I am not a literary genius. I have no creative writing degrees from prestigious schools. I am just a person that has one hell of a story to tell.

If you are reading this, you are getting ready to embark on an epic journey. This novel is the first book in a powerful series. I have spent the better part of a decade developing this story in my head. When I decided to put this story into a book, I never thought I would finish. Now I am compelled to finish telling this story no matter how many books it takes, as I am on the same journey as you, the reader. I am writing this story so that it is told, not for money. If only two people ever read this story from beginning to end, then I have done what I set out to do.

This story is not all sunshine and roses. Parts of it are dark and heart-wrenching to read, but it is even harder to put the book down during those times. I hope that you enjoy this fiction. I pray that it entertains and eventually changes your perspective on the world we live in.

Thank you for reading my story.

Contents

Chapter 1: Good Morning Mr. Rittenhouse 7
Chapter 2: A Dark Side 14
Chapter 3: Two of a kind 23
Chapter 4: 24 Hours Later 30
CHAPTER 5: Shock of it All 48
Chapter 6: The Smell of… 57
Chapter 7: The First Petal 81
Chapter 8: ...And He Appeared Before the Masses 92
Chapter 9: The Soldier 104
Chapter 10: Reality Check 123
Chapter 11: Accepting Fate 147
Chapter 12: Didn't See That Coming 161
Chapter 13: Run Like Hell 176
Chapter 14: The Truth of it All 187
Chapter 15: Meanwhile 195
Chapter 16: A Beer, A Burger and A Story 204
Chapter 17: Burn the Others 217
Chapter 18: Containment 222
Chapter 19: I Love You 227
Chapter 20: Into the Furnaces 244
Chapter 21: The Birth of Malice 251
Chapter 22: Unleash Hell 263
Chapter 23: Fucking Hostile 271
Chapter 24: The Master and the Monster 278

For my wife.
I never would have done this without you.
I love your face.
You really are my dolphin.

Copy Editor
Parker Tinsley

12 Blackened Petals
The Gospel of Sam: Book One

In our ignorance, we thought our only option was to fight. We thought that if we killed him, we would protect ourselves, our way of life. However, it was through this violence that we brought great misery upon ourselves. No one knew that self-preservation would bring such horror to us. Millions died. Millions more were never found.

We did not understand. Our God was not a vengeful God; he just didn't want to be fucked with.

Chapter 1: Good Morning Mr. Rittenhouse

A slow stream of consciousness began to waft through Sam's brain like the smell of bacon that fills the air right before someone eats it all. The ever so vivid dreams that can never be remembered rapidly began to erase themselves as his eyebrows raised just enough to barely crack open his eyelids. It was the start of what promised to be yet another dull as Hell day in the life of Sam Rittenhouse.

He could pretty much map out the day before it began. He would take the next twenty minutes to wrangle himself out of bed, which was not a bed. It was a couch. Sam could neither afford a bed nor did he have a place for a bed in his ultra-tiny apartment. The one room studio apartment was the ultimate in downtown living. Super cramped and small, very expensive and located in an overpriced part of town full of a bunch of well to do, cooler than you, bike riding, beard growing douchebags, or hipsters as they refused to refer to themselves.

This apartment was little more than a room and a closet. It did not even have a kitchen. There were only two plugs. One powered the microwave, which sat on top of an empty mini fridge. The other plug was across the room and remained empty. It was located in the vacant space where Sam imagined there would be a large flat screen TV. The reality of it was that he may never be able to get a flat screen TV or any TV for that matter seeing as he could barely afford rent, or food, or basic hygiene products.

Once he managed to get himself up off the slobber stained, crumb stashing couch, he would wobble his way into the closet. For some reason, in his closet resided a sink, shower and toilet crammed into it. This "closet" listed as a bathroom in the apartment description. They called it, "a spacious bathroom with all the amenities..." but every morning Sam would call bullshit on that. In a still sleepy stupor, he would fumble for a highly overused toothbrush that was broken and duct taped back together like a pair of glasses on some poor egghead's face. The toothbrush would go under the water and into his mouth straight away without any toothpaste.

Sam hated toothpaste and believed it was a conspiracy derived by the government to get people to spend more money on things they didn't need to drive them into poverty; thus making it easier to exert control over the populace. At least, that is what he told himself to feel better about being too poor to afford the simple things that most other Americans took for granted.

Raking the flavorless, worn brush across his teeth, Sam began to contemplate the rest of his day. There were some different options to consider. He knew it was close to noon, and that gave him about 5 hours before his shift started at the restaurant. Five hours of chill before eight hours of Hell. Ideally, he would start the day off by firing up a fresh bowl of super sticky weed before commencing with the day's events, but recreations such as marijuana were also for those with "a silver spoon in their mouths". Instead, he would run some water over his hands and slide his fingers through his short cut, dark brown hair in an attempt to make the severe case of bead head appear somewhat purposeful.

As he made the initial spit of plaque-filled saliva into the sink, he felt the slight twinge of pain that would come like clockwork from a cavity in the far back left molar. Flexing his neck muscles in coordination with squinting his eyes and scrunching his brow, Sam let out a gut wrenching groan. This was the only way he could deal with this annoyance that persisted in killing him for almost a year. He reached back to the sink and grabbed a nearly empty container of Orajel from the spot opposite of where his toothbrush resided. With the precision of a well-oiled machine, he squeezed out the perfect pea sized portion, as recommended by the manufacturer. He then slammed it onto his aching tooth while reciting a quiet internal prayer for the pain to stop.

This sudden onslaught of pain would dictate his actions for the rest of the day before his shift started. Originally, he planned to go and train a little parkour with his longtime friend, Frank. He was itching to get another crack at a gap they were eyeing for quite a while. He bailed the previous three times after making exactly 23 run ups, followed by 23 screams of frustration at not having the balls to follow through on the jump from one roof to the other. These screams are what his friend

Frank referred to as "the mating call of the North American Bitch".

Instead, he would need to have a bit of a relaxed day. He needed a day that would keep his blood pressure and heart rate low. The last thing he wanted to do today was to piss off his tooth and spend the rest of the day with his hand cupped firmly against his cheek. Instead of spending a sweaty day of frustration on some rock-covered rooftop, he would spend the day with the love of his life, Julia.

Julia was a stunning young woman. She was 5 foot 4 inches tall with beautiful locks of flowing black hair. The kind of hair that fell perfectly on her shoulders every day. It was always perfectly styled as though she spent all day with her stylist. Every strand was always in the exact right location, even the ones that fell in front of her beautiful face. They were perfect because it would force here to push it back behind her ear as she looked up at him with those gorgeous brown eyes. They too were also perfect. In fact, Sam could spend an entire day just talking about how perfect everything about her was. He even wrote down and memorized a list of all the things on her that he deemed as "perfect."

The list was up to 243 different things. Many of them were subtle expressions or repetitious actions and habits that any human may have; but to Sam, they were noteworthy and deserved to be not only written down- but also committed to memory. It was his plan to recite all of them to her once he completed that list. However, that may never happen because Sam possessed neither the balls nor the sack that it took to tell Julia that he loved her. In fact, he had not even told her that he liked her in that fashion. He attempted it once while they were in a 3-hour long gaming session. He remembered it so clearly. There she was in sweatpants and a T-shirt, hair pulled back into a ponytail. He was getting his ass handed to him because he could not focus on the game as he was waiting for the right moment. As the words were gearing up in the back of his throat preparing to make their bold and dramatic exit from his lips he received the most crushing blow to the confidence that any potential suitor could ever endure.

He was friend zoned.

Despite popular belief, being friend zoned does not automatically put out the flame of passion in a young man's heart. It only forces him to find clever ways to hide it. As time passes, he would need to make a choice, either hold the flame or extinguish it and move on. He decided that neither of these could be considered suitable answers. Instead, he made the decision to pour gasoline on the fire and refuse to call the fire department. Sam was headstrong with passion. He had never truly been in love before, and he thought that if he was patient and waited for just the right time, he could convince her that he was just the right person for her. She just needed to see that side of him.

Truth be told, Julia always thought he was attractive. She found him funny and witty. He possessed three out of the four credentials that someone needed to capture her romantic interest. Sam knew this. On the front side of his brain, he could not for the life of him figure out why he was friend zoned before he could even get the words out of his mouth. It was a riddle that he needed to solve. How to possess those three amazing traits that she loved so much and leveraged them in his favor for access to her heart. Nevertheless, on the back side of his brain, he knew that a guy needed all four traits before she would allow someone to get close to her in that special way. Moreover, that fourth trait eluded him. It was there in him just as it is in every human being. For some, it is buried just below the surface, for others, it can be buried quite deeply. For Sam, <u>his courage might as well have been buried under the city in a concrete room inside of a stone box.</u> *THE FLOWER: COURAGE*

The benzocaine-laced anesthetic was finally starting to do its job. Sam could feel the pain backing off, and the rhythmic pulse that was pounding in his tooth began to subside. He needed a smoke, and if he was going to catch up to Julia before she started her day, he needed to hustle. He grabbed the same pair of clothes that he was wearing the day before and his backpack and bolted out the door. As he quickly bounced down the stairs, he caught a slight whiff of his armpit. Though he was sure it was him, he felt an overpowering urge to double sniff just for verification. Yep. It was him. This odor was not the kind of smell that would disturb others. This was the kind of smell he would spend the rest of the day wondering if Julia could smell.

"It might just be best to take care of that," he said to himself.

He reached into his bag and pulled out one of the few hygiene products that he owned. The two-year-old stick of Old Spice deodorant lived in his bag for quite some time. The label was marked, worn and tattered but the gel inside still did its job. With a little thought, he stuck the stick under his shirt and into his armpits.

After making himself smell like a 15-year-old boy, he quickly lit the cigarette that was hanging out of his mouth, slung his pack over his shoulder and began his journey through the city. Julia's apartment was only about 12 blocks away. It was a short walk and for a good cause. Not everybody gets to see angels.

She actually is an angel
Murial, AAA

Chapter 2: A Dark Side

Sam loved walking through the city. It was a unique place that was always busy and full of such diversity. You could be as loud as you wanted and no one would care. He could be invisible. These walks always gave him time to think. Time to reflect on the goals and matters at hand and time to reflect on how to repair the cracks in his inner walls before anything else seeped through.

On the outside, Sam appeared to be your average everyday young man. He did not have any strange personality ticks or social abnormalities. If you met him in a bar, you would forget that you even spoke to him. You could describe him as a carbon copy of every other guy you have ever met, but cannot remember. He liked it that way.

For years, he tried to remain relatively invisible and not draw attention to himself. The anonymity allowed him to keep laying brick and mortar on that wall. Just as all of us have, there were secrets behind that wall. However, these were not your average everyday secrets. There were no narcissistic tendencies or strange sexual fetishes behind the wall. It hid no deeply seated racism or overabundant amounts of ego driven desires.

What was behind this wall was something that was far different. It was a thing that desperately wanted to escape. It needed to be seen and heard far more than Sam was able to keep it in. Sam used the strolls through the city to seal those cracks. It was time well spent to see to it that he remained in control of that secret. If there were ever even a small crack left unattended, then that secret could get out, and the whole world would know that Sam was not well.

He was not well at all.

Sam grew up poor. Not just your average poor. The type of poor that makes people bitter. The type of poor that numbs itself with drugs and alcohol. The type poor that surrounds itself with violence and disregard for what is morally and socially right. It brought home a father that was always drunk. The man drank so much that you could smell the alcohol in his sweat every morning. The two-bedroom house that they lived in stunk of the sweaty old alcoholic. The smell permeated every wall of the section 8 home.

If it were not for the benefits they received, Sam would have been homeless and an orphan before he was six years old. His piece of shit father was abusive all the way across the board. He would destroy Sam verbally, emotionally and physically every chance he got. Sam was his punching bag; a chained dog that would get beaten every time he whimpered. If he ever showed any emotion or sense of self-worth, this man would take it from him with foot and fist. Then he would break his spirit even further with a verbal barrage that would test the will of even the strongest drill sergeant. Sam only had one option in life. Take it.

His mother was even worse. She long ago swapped her soul for the soul of a woman who hated everything, including her son. To her, he was the reason she wound up in this mess. He was the reason she was poor and with Sam's shit stain of a father. She would lecture him for hours on end about how crappy her life was and how she wished he would just die so she could be free. This woman was obsessed with her situation and making sure that Sam was acutely aware of how worthless he was. She would take every opportunity to tell him how much he was like his father. Then she would let that self-fueled anger turn into flying fists and feet. Beating Sam was like a sport for her.

His mother and father fought like cats and dogs. They would scream, cuss, and destroy. They would beat each other, and when they finished, they would beat Sam. He hated them with anger that boiled in the back of his throat like tar over a black fire every time he even thought of them. It is likely that few have ever felt that kind of anger. Sam wished he never had. He wanted to hurt them and show them that he was stronger than they were. He was the superior person. He wanted to show them the true power of a chained dog. They needed to feel justice. These shitty people trained him to do this. Keep it in. Do not speak. Just stew in the anger with no outlet. No way to let it go.

Beating Sam was not the only way they showed their dominance over him. Beyond the demeaning and humiliating verbal abuse, and soul-scarring emotional torment that they exerted upon him, there was the box. The box was little more than a shipping crate that his shithead father converted to hold his tools. The box was reinforced to keep it sturdy, but it only held tools for a brief amount of time. The pawnshop would empty it less than a month after its construction. His parents found no trouble finding a use for it. After any given amount of verbal and physical pounding, Sam got thrown in the box.

At two feet wide, eighteen inches tall and five feet long, this box was smaller than a coffin. Dirt and rust with various nuts and old nails filled the bottom of the box. They would lock the top and leave him for hours, sometimes days. The long hours in the box would not pass by quickly. The roaches that came in and out of the box were very curious and seemed to explore everything. As if being trapped in this small confined space was not bad enough, there was no water, nor food, nor bathroom breaks.

This was torture. This was Hell.

The only relief that Sam ever got was at school. He was able to escape the torment of his captors for at least eight hours. Truthfully, it wasn't too much of a reprieve. He was poor, and that made him a target. Everything about him made him a target. His shabby clothing and shaggy appearance were a constant point of attack for the more fortunate students that attended his school. It was always the kids that knew the joys of financial and social privilege that launched the attacks. He would listen to the endless procession of taunts the other students flung at him from hallways and schoolyards. He was the topic of conversation for the kids that got picked on when they needed to feel better about themselves. However, at least, it was not as bad as what he endured at home.

The girls in his school were unapproachable. He simply did not exist in their eyes. Sam didn't have the nerve to bother talking to them. He learned from his parents that he was not worth a damn. That seemed to follow suit with what his biology teacher said about women genetically seeking strength, safety and comfort in a mate. He could offer none of the three. Besides, even if he did manage to muster up the gall to speak to a member of the opposite sex, he did not have the patience to deal with the bitchy "McCunty" attitude they all developed towards him. After a long day of ridicule by his peers and being ignored by the girls, he would head home to the place he hated most of all. Out of the frying pan and into the fire.

He hated his life. He hated himself. Breathing was not worth the effort it required.

As if this was not bad enough, Sam was required to see a therapist twice a week. The court ordered it, and it was paid for by the state. Therapy was the only thing his parents let him do on his own. It kept the government benefits flowing into the house. He had no choice. His sessions became mandatory after his family received a visit from a social worker. The worker could see that things were not right and that Sam was miserable. She could find no way to prove that there was abuse in the home. The parents were amazing actors and Sam was far too terrified to speak up about what was going on in the house.

Mrs. Winters was a kind but stern woman who had seen it all. As a social worker, she could read the lies on people's faces and was good at finding ways to help children. She pulled Sam aside for a private conversation with the tormented young boy; prodding Sam for the real info on what was happening in that poor excuse for a family home. He would not say a word about what his parents were doing to him. He avoided that portion of the conversation altogether. He did, however, mention that he was having the worst dreams. The kind that would make him sweat profusely. Often he would wake up with his sheets so soaked in sweat that he would think he pissed his pants. A couple of times it scared him so bad that he did.

Mrs. Winters saw this as a legitimate opportunity to get him some help. She often said to her fellow social workers that sometimes the best medicine for an ailing heart was an open ear. She could not have been more right.

Sam was referred to a therapist. His therapist was a young man, in his early thirties. Magnificently talented, but still paying his dues by doing social work until he saved enough money and accolades to start his practice. His name was Dr. Steven Wallace, and he took a keen interest in this young man from such a broken home. Sam would do everything he could to stay in Dr. Wallace's office and keep the conversation going. He was the one person Sam could open up to and the only person he would tell about his dreams. Dr. Wallace was also the only one that was allowed to see what was lurking deep inside of Sam. He was the one that laid the first bricks in the wall.

Over the years that he visited Dr. Wallace, Sam described in detail how horrifying, and real his dreams were. He talked at great length about a fiery place that reeked of sulfur and ash. He talked about the black sludge that trapped him there and about the thing that he would fear every time he was there.

He described it as a monster that he knew lived there, but he could not see. It would speak to him, but he could never understand it. It would torment him by binding him to massive plates of rock and smoldering stone while showing him horrific images of people suffering. Images that would sear into his mind, and stay there. He thought that this was what crazy people saw. He believed it to be his dark side and he called it by the word that would be on his tongue when he awoke from the dream.

Malice.

Malice tormented him every time he fell asleep. There was no escape.

Dr. Wallace attributed the dreams to the rough life that Sam was experiencing. Though he never said a word about the violence at home, he carried all the telltale traits of a severely abused child. This, in turn, carried with it all the troubles of mental illness. The dreams were Sam's way of coping with the darkness that surrounded him. At least, that is what the good doctor thought at first.

If only he were right.

By the age of 15, Sam slipped into a state of full-blown depression. There was no light at the end of the tunnel. No silver linings to any cloud. There was only darkness.

The abuse at home reached an all-time high. The bullying at school persisted and grew throughout the years, and there was no end in sight. The dreams became far more vivid and violent. All he wanted was out. By this time, there were two failed suicide attempts. The scars on his wrist were a sign of one. He cut them the wrong way and did not have the guts to go deep enough. They only bled for about 10 minutes.

The second was a botched hanging. He decided not to go through with it at the last minute but slipped off the chair. After just seconds of struggling, the cord broke loose of its anchor and Sam came crashing down on his ass. He couldn't even get it right if he wanted to. It seemed for a while that Sam's fate was to remain in Hell.

A breath of fresh air came to him one night in the form of a lung full of smoke. Sam's house was set ablaze. He was the only survivor. Though never confirmed, the authorities believed that his drunk ass father passed out with a cigarette in his hand. Incredibly groggy, Sam awoke in the hallway only feet from the front door. He didn't have a clue how he made it there, but he was happy to be alive. There was not a single effort from him to help save his parents from the fire. As he arduously made his way to the door, he could faintly hear his mother scream in agony, and then the screaming stopped. A light ignited at the end of the tunnel once more, and it was a bright orange. Sam stumbled outside and collapsed on the ground.

Sam spent the next three years in juvenile homes and therapy. Eventually, Sam began to smile, and the wall he was building grew thick and strong. He was able to bury the demons of his past, at least somewhat. Upon his eighteenth birthday, they released him from custody and began a life of independence anew.

Chapter 3: Two of a kind

The third floor, right at the end of the hall and 4th door on the left. He could find his way to it blindfolded. The first time he came here, he made sure to memorize exactly where this was. Julia's apartment has always been in the same place, at least for the five years that he had known her.
He could still remember the first time they met quite vividly. It was on the staircase in front of the building. She was sitting there reading a book that was way above his reading level. That perfectly dark hair pulled back in a ponytail. Glasses on. Julia did not need a prescription. They were a fashion statement that she was trying out at the time.

She was the type of girl that was beautiful to everyone but seemed unobtainable to the dorky boys. She wore them in an attempt to attract a less douche baggy type of guy. It worked. She attracted many dorky boys; the only problem was that they did not have the confidence to come and talk to her. Confidence was a very important thing for her. A lack of confidence was a lack of courage. Moreover, without courage, you might as well not even bother.

Around the corner from the alley came Sam. He had been running this line since he moved into the neighborhood. Around the corner, hop up onto the rail, jump to the other rail on the opposite side of the stairs and tear out of there. However, that day was a bit different. The sudden appearance of Sam from nowhere bounding up onto something that was not meant to be stood on ripped her attention from her book.

Sam hopped up onto the rail without even noticing her, jumped to the rail on the opposite side of the staircase. Sam became so confident with this maneuver, in this location, that he took it for granted that he would do this the same every time. Midway through his jump, he noticed the beautiful girl watching him from his peripheral vision and lost concentration. This momentary lack of focus changed his approach on the landing. Instead of landing on top of it, he essentially did a double-footed kick to the side of it. The rail gave way at the base and went flying. Sam fell like a sack of potatoes.

The first thing to hit the ground was his hand. It folded his right forearm into a 90-degree angle. Julia heard the break. It was quite a gruesome sound. Kind of like the sound of breaking a stick of celery mixed with the sound of squishing raw hamburger in the palm of your hand, as she would later describe it. Before he could even feel the pain, his head smacked the concrete.

Lights out.

Sam slowly peeled his eyes open. Caught completely off guard by his surroundings, he knew he was in a hospital room. The fogginess in his head did not mask a dull pain in his arm and a tremendous pounding in his head. A quick and groggy survey of the room revealed a few things. This place was not the emergency room; it was a regular room, which meant that he was there for at least one night, or they were keeping him for one night. There was an IV in his arm, and that was the potential source of the loopy feeling. His other arm was in a cast, which meant that whatever happened to him broke his arm. He did not check himself into the hospital, and he did not remember calling the paramedics, so someone brought him to this hospital, most likely an ambulance. Finally, there was a stunningly beautiful woman sitting in the chair beside his bed. He had absolutely no idea who she was, but it was the first sight that he saw since he woke up that was worth a damn.

"Are you okay?" She asked softly.

Her voice was like that of an angel; he thought to himself. Such a beautiful girl asking a question like that in such a silky voice required an eloquent response. However, the drugs prevented such a suave phrase to be passed from his lips. Instead, his statement was far less eloquent.

"Fuck my head hurts," The words seeped out of his mouth like some barely intelligible dribble. The painkillers clouded every ounce of intelligence that was swirling through his brain. He could barely form cohesive thoughts at this point. The three that he could muster up at that point were:

My head hurts. Damn, she's hot. I sound like an idiot.

And not necessarily in that order.

He would spend the next few days in that hospital bed recovering from his fall. The cracked skull and broken arm would heal nicely, and the beautiful woman would keep him company through those days. Sam would continually remark to the striking young lady that beautiful women should not be spending their days hanging out with broken people in hospital rooms. She would just laugh and shrug off the compliment. He couldn't figure out why she stayed.

As the weeks and months passed, Julia kept Sam in constant company. She would always seek him out and have fun things to do. Even though he could recognize her advances and yearned for her company in a more romantic way, he never could summon the balls to do anything about it. Maybe it was the years of violence that beat him into submission. Maybe he just needed to wait until the right time. Maybe he was just a coward.

Regardless of the reason, it was his inability to say anything to her about the way he felt that doomed him to the friend zone. After the years of late night hangouts and video game marathons, he just could not bring himself to utter those three words that would change their status to something other than friends.

His trip down memory lane was at an end. Sam stood in front of her door; hand in the air ready to do the same rhythmic knock he always did. He stood there for what seemed like an eternity, debating whether today would be the day he would spill his guts to her. However, this decision today would end the same way it did every time he stood in this doorway. First, he would psych himself up and raise his hand to knock on the door with his head held high, and just before he would knock that voice in his head would chime in.

"You're not good enough to even be around a girl like this. You are a worthless piece of shit that pollutes the air every time you speak. Give up now and save yourself the embarrassment."

It was the voice of his mother and father. The voice that told him girls like that didn't like guys like him. They liked strong men, not weak little boys. That voice would tell him that he was truly worthless and that if he loved her, he would stay out of the way and let her find a real man; not a worthless piece of shit like him. By the time the voice was done, it had sounded just like his voice. A voice that he could believe and trust. A voice that would have no problem convincing him that he did not stand a chance, and there was no reason to try even.

Sam's head dropped, and his gaze fell to the floor. He made his decision.

"I am a coward." he mumbled to himself.

A wave of self-loathing flowed through him as it did every time he refused to make the decision to fight for what was right. He realized a long time ago that even though he felt this way most of the time, the day must continue and he needed to continue with it.

It was time to put on the mask again. It was a mask that he constructed for himself. It was two sided. On the outside, it showed a happy face. A face that showed the world he was a well-adjusted and happy human being. It said that he enjoyed the presence of others and put his dark past behind him.

"Sure I am happy and yes I would love a latte."

The inside of the mask was dramatically different; this side faced him. It could see what was really in his soul. It knew his scars, and it was always telling him that he was worthless. Every time he put on the mask, it reminded him of the things that he refused to let anyone see. The anger. The hatred. The shame and sorrow. The mask represented a mark of slavery to the very people that made him this way.

He hated that damn mask.

Raising his head, he created the perfect fake smile and knocked. There was no answer. He knocked again, still no answer. Turning his ear toward the door, he hoped to catch a faint sound coming from inside that would warrant him knocking a third time. There was no such sound.

"Damn" he whispered quietly to himself.

The one thing he wanted to do today slipped through his fingers. Sam was not the type of person to be bored and, for him, time doing nothing was time wasted. Since he could not do what he wanted to do, he was going to do what he didn't want to do.

He was going to have to jump that damn gap. Time to find Frank.

Chapter 4: 24 Hours Later

This again. He thought he would never wind up here after the last time. In fact, it had been almost five years since he was here. He hated this place. Everything about it was uncomfortable and painful. Especially when he first got here. It was as if he went through the same bullshit every time.

He didn't like a single thing about this horrid hole in the middle of wherever. Everything here sucked, but the pit was the worst; and unfortunately, it was the only way in or out. He didn't come here by choice. He always just wound up here, like he was drug in here. As soon as he closed his eyes and fell asleep, he would wake up in this Hell. The pit was such a horrid place because of the dredge and slime that filled it. It was nearly impossible to move through and coated every inch of him as if he took a swan dive into the stuff. He would spend what felt like hours just trying to get out of this godforsaken, shithole pit.

The thick black mixture looked like oil and moved like tar. It covered his entire face; all but one eye. He couldn't even breathe. The first few times he was here he was struck down by sheer panic. There are many horrible things in this world, but not being able to take in a lung full of air was one of the worst. Normally one would just pass out, but in here, not needing to breath is not a means of escape. This was just one of the tortures awaiting Sam in this Hell.

The absolute amount of effort that he needed to exert to pull himself from the sludge was enough to break most people into tears. By the time he got out, that is exactly what he was doing…crying. He hated the struggle of freeing himself from that goddamned pit. The smell of that disgusting sludge would stick to him like glue. He knew that when he finally woke up from this nightmare, that smell would become plastered inside of his nostrils like a thick layer of snot he just couldn't get out.
This dream was not just some random firing of his sleeping brain. His nightmarish Hell was a nightly torture for most of his childhood.

Nothing changed about this place. The sky was still black as smoke. The heat was like standing in a fire, and it created massive gusts of searing wind that would blow the still burning embers that filled the air right into his face. His eyes always felt as if they started to cook inside of his skull. The fire destroyed everything here. No matter what the scenery was, it looked as though it were rusting in a fiery kiln for decades. This particular time it was the cityscape outside of his apartment, but it was always somewhere different. As if a snapshot was taken of the world around him and the set ablaze to burn for all eternity. Some things never change.

Sam called this place The Furnaces.

He was completely lucid in these dreams though he did not have the kind of control most would expect to get from a truly lucid experience. He could not fly or instantly acquire super strength. His body was bound to the physics of this world. Sam simply retained his logical mind in here; however, there was no escaping his emotions.

After years of very intensive therapy, he was able to escape this madness. The wall he built held strong and steady against the constant push of that dark bastard that lived behind it.

Until now.

Sam always heard muffled voices in the dream, but this dream was the first time he ever heard intelligible words. This voice was unlike any other he heard here before. Its power washed out all the other sounds that usually deafened him in this Hellish dream.

With a mighty, thunderous voice, it said, "All that power is pointless unless you can control it."

These words seemed to pound on the walls of Sam's head as he made the screaming ascent into consciousness. They pounded so hard in his mind that they reverberated against his ears as he gasped for air, sitting straight up from his coma-like sleep. The discombobulation that often accompanies waking up at such a rapid rate was not there. In fact, Sam was never more aware of anything in his entire life.

He could feel every drop of sweat on his brow brought

on by his vision filled sleep. Each drop possessed a unique shape and personality of its own. He could taste the funk of plaque and night-old spit that has hung in his mouth as well as the thick humid air that rushed over his tongue as it filled his lungs with rapid deep breaths. The tips of his fingers were so keenly aware of every divot in the pattern that covered the microfiber pillows so tightly clutched in his palms that he knew how many there were touching his hand and how deep they were. Two hundred nineteen on the left and one hundred ninety-six on the right are each one-sixty-fourth of an inch deep.

As the sounds of his dreams began to fade into the abyss of his subconscious, new sounds overwhelmed his ears. The world around him instantly divided into several audible layers like that of the rain forest as you descend through the canopy. At first, all he could hear was the roar of the traffic three floors below as it penetrated its way through the balcony door. The crushing sound of rubber on concrete and combustion engines rattling and revving as they accelerated through the intersection trying to beat the yellow light. The thud of a car with heavy subwoofer mounted so poorly that it rattled the trunk. The splash of tires as they caressed the edge of the puddles gathered along the curbs from the previous night's storm.

As the seconds passed, he could hear faint glimpses of conversations from the outdoor patio of the hipster coffee shop across the street and the click of high heels walking hurriedly past as if in a rush to return to work.

Sam released his lock-tight grip on the upholstery and

placed his hands on the sides of his face, fingers covering his eyes, and he began to rub them slowly in an attempt to "get a grip" on what seemed still to be a dream. But this was no dream and the reality that was invading him was about to get worse.

As he pulled his fingers from his eyes and his hands from his face he muttered "Two thousand sixty-three whiskers, nine thousand fourteen pores and a whole lot of WHAT THE FUCK!!!!!"

His eyes bulged open in complete disbelief at what just flew out of his mouth. Then it got very bad.
Gazing down at the carpet below his feet, he could see each fiber as though he was looking at the world's highest definition television with a magnifying glass. He could see the follicles of the hairs that were growing out of his legs, dirt particles encrusted on the fabric of the shorts that he slept in and the coagulated cells of the blood that stained his shirt.

Sam lost it. Almost as quickly as he could think it, he rushed down the hall and into the bathroom. Crashing into the tiny sink mounted below the tiny mirror so hard that it cracked away from the wall, knocking all of his toiletries off the edges that they so delicately balanced on. He rammed into it so hard in fact that his tiny mirror fell into that very same sink and shattered into dozens of pieces. The sound was so deafening that Sam immediately clutched his ears and stumbled back screaming, "FUCK!"

Shaking his head, he leaned forward toward the sink again and reached in to grab a piece of the tiny mirror that was now much miniature than before.

As he did so, he mumbled, "Thirty-seven pieces too small...28th should work."

The sliver that he chose was the largest piece in the pile and was indeed the twenty-eighth piece from the bottom of the sink. He raised the sliver of mirror up in front of his face and once again bulged his eyes in disbelief at what he was seeing. His eyes changed color and pattern. Normally his eyes were a soft brown. They, of course, had a distinct pattern like everyone else's eyes but if you didn't own his eyes or spend your days staring at them like some star-crossed lover you would have never noticed any pattern at all. Nevertheless, Sam knew what that pattern looked like and today it was different.

The color changed to a yellowish gold. Not that of a poisonous snake or possessed alley cat, but an alluring, almost soothing gold with yellow highlights radiating from the center around the pupil. The pattern was nothing short of perfect. It was a series of nine tiny circles, equidistant from each other as well as the pupil. In between each pair of circles was a perfect black sliver that guided ones focus back towards the pupil. Even Sam felt slightly hypnotized by them.

His disbelief grew even more. In an emotionless gesture, he dropped the sliver of the tiny mirror back into the sink. Upon impact, it broke again.

"Forty-three pieces," rolled off his lips as though he did not even want himself to hear it.

He closed his eyes slowly. He stood up straight and took in a deep calming breath, placed his hands on the edge of the sink and sank his weight, leaning forward. Again, he could sense a tremendous amount of information. He could feel that the temperature of the porcelain was a cool sixty-four point seven degrees as his hands settled on the smooth surface. He could see each bit of grit, dirt and soap scum that appeared glued to the sink from the six weeks that he occupied this apartment. Random whiskers that had not made it down the drain from the last hack shave job a few days ago were clearly visible. He exhaled and slowly opened his eyes, looking down into the sink he hoped and prayed that he would see himself looking back up from the tiny broken mirror, not these strange and unfamiliar eyes, but the soft pattern less brown eyes that he had known for the past twenty-three years. This was not the case. What Sam saw were forty-three pairs of those golden yellow eyes staring back at him with the same unanswered question of, "What the fuck?"

It was all just a bit too much for this young man to handle at noon-thirty on a Monday morning. His young but extremely masculine, square jaw clinched and the muscle tensed causing the whiskers on his face to conform to its shape. His grip on the edge of the sink increased exponentially causing the porcelain to burst under the vice-like force, sending shards ricocheting off the walls and porcelain powder puffing into the air.

"SON OF A..." Sam shouted from behind his tight-clenched teeth. He began shaking his hands vigorously and bouncing up and down ever so slightly, "FUCKING OOOWWWWW!"

Apparently Sam's sense of pain was amplified as well. He immediately opened his hands, palms facing upward, and began to survey the damage on his now bleeding hands. He could see the dust and leftover debris of the sink that was still stuck to his hands in magnified, crystal clear detail. He could see several lacerations to the palms of his hands. Each was deep. Deep and nasty. As he began to focus harder, he could see that the wounds were already repairing themselves. The cells that were rushing to the wound to begin the coagulation process were apparent and vivid. Barely visible capillaries already began to constrict. Sam could not help but feel like he was watching some time lapse of the entire process. What was even worse was that he noticed a startling resemblance between the blood on his hands and the blood on his shirt. The pain began to subside.

He reached up to the wall next to where the tiny mirror resided a few moments earlier, grabbed what was no doubt a very non-sterile hand towel, wrapped it around his left hand, and clenched the end of it into his palm to hold it in place. He grabbed a second towel with his right hand and simply squeezed it. He always heard you should apply pressure to open wounds, but Sam thought that was stupid as hell because right now his hands were stinging like a son of a bitch from the towels and the pressure.

He leaned back against the wall, dropped his head slightly and looked toward the ground. Giggled in a sort of slightly deranged fashion and said, "Five hundred fourteen squares."

He was referring to the pattern of the cheap vinyl flooring of the bathroom in his shitty studio apartment.

All he could think was, "I need a smoke."

Without hesitation, he exited the now destroyed tiny bathroom, grabbed his cigarettes and lighter off the cluttered coffee table he got from the back alley and headed for the door.

Upon entering the hallway, his senses overwhelmed him again. The normally disgusting smell of the overly sweaty alcoholic that lived across the hallway was far more intense and seemed to stain the inside of his nostrils instantly. It was a smell he knew all too well from his childhood. Caught completely off guard, Sam paused for a brief moment as though he were trying to hold back the worst puke ever. Then he wretched. Placing his hand over his mouth in a fist shape, he decided that he needed out of this hallway and fast.

Upward was salvation. Upward was fresh air.

Moments later Sam reached the top of the sixth-floor staircase. He dug into the almost empty pack of smokes and pulled out a cigarette, being careful not to grab the lucky one that he flipped upside down in the pack. He put the butt in between his lips and drove his shoulder into the beaten red door to open it. Almost as if never connected, the door flew off the hinges and traveled some 10 feet away from the frame itself. The flimsy, metal door landed with a crash that was thunderous and loud even to the average person. For Sam, it was almost crippling. Once again, he drove his hands up to his ears and hunched over in pain. As if it was not bad enough already, the light from the mid-day sun rushed into the dark stairwell, filling the dank corridor with more light than his eyes were prepared to handle. Pain seemed to be the common theme of the day. Pain and confusion.

Gathering himself, he stood up straight and raised the back of his towel wrapped hand to his forehead in an attempt to shade his eyes from the blisteringly bright sun that felt like it was searing his retinas. Staggeringly, he exited the stairwell and stepped out onto the rooftop. Sam came here to smoke five or six times a day. It was his thinking spot, his hidden place away from the rest of the world. The one place that never changed for him no matter how bad things got. The one place he knew he could truly be alone.

Today, however, nothing was as it should have been. With his pupils finally constricting and offering him the slightest bit of relief from the overpowering sun, Sam fumbled with his lighter trying to get it to light, but with no luck. He shook it vigorously a few times and tried again. Just as he managed to get a flame and bring it to the tip of the cigarette, he heard a voice in the place where there should not be voices.

"I wouldn't do that if I were you," the voice said.

In true smoker fashion, Sam lit the cigarette and inhaled deeply with the intention of replying on the exhale. Nicotine first, all else second.

Sam began to cough so violently that he sounded like the car from earlier with the poorly installed subwoofers that made the trunk rattle. Saliva streamed from the rim of his mouth and began to drip on the ground. There was no controlling this. The coughing seemed to go on for about a minute or so and involved Sam puking before he was able to calm himself enough to ask, "Who the Hell are you?"

Not interested in the answer, Sam stood there, straight legged and bent at the waist, hands on his knees, still coughing a bit. Standing before him was a well-dressed man. He wore a lightweight brown herringbone jacket with the collar popped and the sleeves rolled up to reveal the bright white shirt below.

The sleeves were just a bit longer than they needed to be. Holes were punched in the cuffs and the man's thumbs were sticking through, making a pseudo glove. His pants were a regular fit faded denim that broke slightly at the ankles. His shoes appeared broken in, black leather loafers with a square front. They were the kind of shoe that you pay a lot of money for so they look worn when you buy them new.

Atop this six-foot-tall, sharply dressed figure was a head that would make even the most heterosexual man say, "Damn, that dude is sexy."

The five o'clock shadow and perfectly swept blonde hair only seemed to compliment the penetrating vivid blue eyes, sculpted nose, and square jaw.

The man extended his right hand to shake Sam's and said, "I'm Michael, your recorder."

"My what?" replied Sam snidely as he raised up to eye level with Michael and wiped a bit of drool from his lips.

"Your recorder," said Michael, "it'll make sense in a few minutes."

With one eyebrow raised and his nose all scrunched up, Sam said, "I'm not a musician, and I don't need anything recorded buddy. I can't help you." He spoke to the man as if he were turning down a bum on the street that was asking for change. Sam began to reach for his cigarette that was lying on the rooftop still smoking from the coughing fit he went through just a moment ago. Clearing his throat, he pinched it between his fingertips and raised it towards his lips when Michael interrupted once more.

"Are you seriously going to do that again?"

Sam placed the smoke in between his lips to the right side and squinted his right eye to prevent the smoke from getting in.

"What are you? The fucking cigarette police? Trying to keep me from killing myself? No offense, but you should just let me smoke in peace and give me some space, man," Sam rattled off.

Almost as if he were reading a quote from the most well-known story in the world, Michael replied with an emotionless response, "You couldn't kill yourself even if you wanted to, and you are stuck with me for the rest of your life."

With a single sarcastic forced laugh, Sam said, "Is that so?"

He took another drag off the cigarette and proceeded to re-live the horrendous coughing fit from only a few moments ago.

While scratching the back of his head with his right hand, Michael said with the slightest hint of frustration, "Look, I don't feel like wasting most of the day trying to convince you that what I've got to say is real.... So I am just going to show you...Cool?"

Once again, in the smokers hacking position, bent over,

and head down, drooling, Sam raised his towel wrapped hand out in front of him in an agreeing fashion. A gesture that said "Sure thing, but fuck off."

Michael said, "Fabulous." and rushed into Sam's personal space faster than the normal person could perceive. Sam saw the entire action in slow motion. He was so stunned by what was happening that he could not react. He had never been in a fight before. He had his ass kicked constantly, but was never allowed to defend himself and never dealt with confrontation like this. For his first encounter, this was off the charts. Michael grabbed him by the collar and by the leg of his shorts, lifted him off the ground, and as if throwing a bale of hay, spun 360 degrees before tossing Sam from the rooftop. Sam, still paralyzed from the shock and awe of what was happening did not fall to the ground.

Michael threw him so hard and with such force that Sam rocketed out instead of down. He flew from his rooftop beyond the apartment building next to him and came crashing down like a sack of potatoes on the rooftop of a four-story apartment building some two-hundred-fifty feet away. Trailing only a split second behind him was Michael soaring through the air in an angelic fashion. Like something out of *The Matrix*, Michael landed on the roof while Sam was still tumbling like a rag doll. Casually, Michael strolled towards Sam.

Gasping for air, Sam rolled onto his back, only to see Michael towering above him. The Sun was blasting out from behind his head like some painting in the Sistine

Chapel.

Looking down at Sam with eyes that glowed like ice blue sapphires, Michael spoke in a booming, authoritative voice, "I am the Archangel Michael, created for Ra, the Sixth replacement of this world. I am here to record everything you do for the rest of your 11 lives. I have been alive for eleven thousand three hundred and sixty-four years. I cannot die. You cannot kill me."

Michael reached down and once again grabbed Sam by the collar of his shirt. He raised him to his feet without a single drop of effort and said, "People are going to try to kill you over and over, and no matter how hard you try, they will succeed, and you will die again and again. I am here to watch."

With a look of utter confusion and disbelief, Sam gazed at Michael. His inability to speak clued Michael in on Sam's mental state. Maybe his approach was a bit too abrupt. Maybe Sam was having some serious emotional problems at the moment. From the look in his eyes, he checked out.

"Sam! Hey..." Michael began snapping his fingers in front of Sam's face "...you in there? If you are, you need to get it together man."

Michael pursed his lips to the side slightly and cocked one eye towards the ever so stunned young man in front of him.

"Humph...utterly pathetic. Five thousand years together and I get dumped for this moron". With a sigh he leaned back slightly, still keeping one eye on Sam's' scared and lifeless expression. "Well, guess it can't be helped."

Michael drew back with his right hand. He reached so far back that his fingertips almost touched the rooftop, and in a fashion that would have made Kat Williams proud, he swung that hand forward and pimp slapped Sam so hard that it took him off his feet. Once again, Sam tumbled like a rag doll. After finally tumbling to a stop, Sam lifted himself up to his knees and spit the blood from his mouth.

"You hit like a bitch," Sam grumbled as he peered out at Michael from underneath his eyebrows.

In an instant, Sam exploded towards Michael. He moved faster than any Olympic sprinter could ever dream. He went from catatonic to full on a rampage in the blink of an eye and the rage on his face was apparent. Moving forward with the force of a wrecking ball and the speed of a cheetah, Sam collided with Michael and took him off his feet. There was so much force and speed behind his action that he drove Michael into the wall of the brick elevator housing that was on the far side of the roof. The two collided into the wall with a tremendous thud and sent cracks rippling through the red brick structure.

"WHOOOOOO!" Shouted Michael as he dawned an

overly exhilarated grin on his face, completely unfazed by the massive impact he just sustained at Sam's hands.

"So that's why he chose you! You are all piss, and vinegar aren't you?" said Michael as he widened his eyes in excitement.

"What is wrong with me?" Growled Sam. "Why is this happening to me?"

He gave Michael a little extra shove into the already cracked wall causing small bits of brick and dust to crumble away. The intensity filled Sam's eyes along with tears of frustration.

His teeth clenched tight as he shouted from behind them, "ANSWER ME!"

Bits of drool flew from the edges of his lips as he gave Michael one more solid shove. This one was enough to break the wall and send Michael through it. Landing on his back, still giggling, the rubble from the now smashed and broken brick wall piled on top of him. It was only a moment before the Archangel was standing up and brushing the rubble from his well-polished exterior. With a few final pats and brushes to remove the dust from himself, he placed his hands on his lapels, adjusted his coat, and popped his collar.

"There is nothing wrong with you..." he said with pure confidence, "you are perfect, or at least on your way to perfection. It's all just part of the process."

"Stop fucking with me!" barked Sam as he fell to his knees, driving the heels of his hands to his forehead as if he were trying to crush his skull. Sam broke down into tears.

He said, "Just tell me what is going on. How did this happen?"

"You honestly don't remember? I swear you are worse than he was." Michael sighed and raised his eyebrows for a second. He extended his hand and said, "Take my hand, and I'll Show you how this happened. But I am warning you; you won't like the answer."

Sam reached up and grabbed Michael's hand as if he were shaking it.

"Get ready for one hell of a flashback." Michael closed his eyes and whispered something completely unintelligible.

Sam's eyes rolled back into his head as he slumped forward lifelessly onto his knees.

Chapter 5: Shock of it All

Sam's mind slipped into a flashback from twenty-four hours earlier.

He stood on the roof of a building he had been looking at for weeks. He was studying it with special attention to the proximity of its neighbor. He was trying to size up the distance from one rooftop to the other. From the ground, it looked like ten feet. Also, it appeared that this building was about a five or six-foot height difference. Sam kept telling himself that this would be a piece of cake. He could totally make the distance. All he would need is about a twenty foot run up, and he could easily make the jump to the next building. At least, that is what he had been telling himself for weeks.

Standing on top of the monstrous building and looking at the gap from this perspective changed his tune. The reality of it all was that the gap was about fifteen feet across and almost twelve feet higher than the roof on which he would land. He knew that he could technically make the gap. Sam's training in parkour was at the four-year mark, and he held a firm grip on what needed to happen. If everything went according to plan, he would just make it beyond the edge and roll out. That was if everything went according to plan.

Sam's mind was racing faster than his heart.

"This should be a simple jump," he thought.
However, when there is risk involved, the mind starts to wander off track. What if his jump was weak or his foot slipped? Heaven forbid he fell short by only a few inches. After all, he was ten stories up. You do not get back up from a fall like that.

To make matters worse, he was here with his best friend, Frank, who was ranting the entire way about how famous they would be for jumping this gap. All of their friends would envy them and try to copy it. For just a brief second the thought of backing out crossed his mind. His gut told him to listen to that thought, but his pride simply would not allow it. Besides, Frank was already on the other side. He successfully made the jump, and Sam could not risk appearing like that much of a bitch.

This was it. Do or die. The decisive moment. Sam sucked in all the bravery and breath his lungs could handle. With a powerful exhale, he darted toward the edge of the building. As he reached full sprint, he realized that there was no turning back. He was running way too fast to stop before the edge. The only option now was a full commitment. He poured on the steam and mustered up all his power. Sam reached the edge and planted his foot on the lip. The grip of the brick below his shoe was solid; the power in his quads and calf muscles was explosive as he launched himself confidently towards the adjacent roof.

"I got this!" he thought.

Time seemed to slow down for Sam. The first half of the jump was breathtaking. To be so high, in such a vulnerable position with no way out…this is where the rush came from. The second half of the jump was not as dreamy and prolific. Right around the half way point, Sam realized that he did not jump out far enough. He jumped high instead of long. But when you are floating in mid-air, there is nothing you can do.

With a ferocious scream at the top of his lungs, Sam stretched his arms out in a last ditch effort to save himself. He needed to get his hands on that ledge. He couldn't be the guy all splattered at the bottom of this building. How would it look if the news was there showing his body all spattered on the ground? How would he ever get laid if he was dead? He must grab the ledge.

Sam never was a lucky person. He never won any bet. He never got the girl or saved the day. In fact, if it were not for bad luck he would not have any luck at all. But today was different. Somehow, Sam managed to grab the ledge. As he came screaming out of the sky from the edge of the other building he so daringly leaped from, he managed to put his hands on the ledge and hang on. Keeping his grip was no easy task. The sheer force of his weight falling from that far felt as though it were going to rip his arms from their sockets. His chest and knees slammed into the side of the building so hard that it knocked the wind from his lungs and felt as though it broke both kneecaps.

But he grabbed the ledge. He was going to live. For how long was yet to be determined. His grip was fading fast and smashing into the wall didn't help. He could feel the damage done to the skin on his hands even though he couldn't see it and he knew that climbing was going to be beyond difficult. He felt the powerful grip of Frank's hand wrap around his wrist and then the other one.

"I got you." Frank's voice never sounded so good.

Sam looked up and saw the face of his friend. His only real friend. His partner in crime. Frank was a young-looking man in his early twenties. His hair was medium length, brown, gelled up in the perfect emo style. Sweeping from the back of his head and spiky in the front. Intentionally messy, almost boy band-ish. Like Sam, his eyes were soft brown, and it appeared as though there was a bit of Latino in him, visibly diluted by a few generations. His skin was dark from a long summer of training shirtless in the sun, and his body was devoid of any hair.

Even his face was smooth. He could go for a week without shaving, and it would look like he shaved that morning. He was strong. A medium sized tattoo stretched across the top portion of his chest just below the collarbone. It was a word written in old English style lettering done in black with gray shading. It said, "Benjamin$." The "s" was made out to look like a dollar sign. There was no doubt about it, Frank's number one focus in life was money.

With a look of strain on his face, Frank began to hoist Sam up onto the rooftop. Sam's face shared a similar look of strain. He struggled to get traction to assist Frank in the climbing effort. Once he reached the top, Sam laid flat on his back and stared at the sky for a second trying to process what just happened. He cheated death. He knew it. Without saying a single word, he reached into his pocket and pulled out a soft pack of cigarettes. Slapping his hands together, he tapped one out and placed it between his lips. Dropped the pack on the rooftop and fished a lighter out of his pocket, struck it, lit his smoke and breathed in deeply.

"You know those things are gonna kill you right?" Frank scolded. Sam exhaled his lung full of smoke, sat up and gave Frank the eat-shit-and-die look.

"I almost died right there, dude," Sam said as he pointed at the ledge of death from which he just returned, "I'm not stressing a fucking cigarette."

"But you've got to admit that was fucking EPIC, yo. I thought you were done for dude," Frank said with the most glorious grin on his face. "You should have seen the look on your face bro. Are you sure you didn't shit yourself? Cause I would've," He proclaimed.

Sam calmly replied, "I would rather we just not talk about that for a bit, my hands are shaking. I just need to cool out for a moment."

Frank frowned and raised his eyebrows while shaking his head in agreement, "I can respect that. If I just shit my pants, I wouldn't want to talk about it either."

Sam gracefully raised his middle finger to shoot Frank the bird.

Laughing slightly, Frank questioned, "You think about that gig I was telling you about yesterday? That shit's tonight man and I need a partner."

Sam raised himself off the ground and walked back over to the edge. He looked down and said, "Nah bro, I've got to work tonight."

Sam could almost see himself splattered on the ground. He imagined people just walking around him as if he didn't matter.

"Work?!?" Frank snapped back in disgust, "do this job with me tonight and you make almost as much as you do all year at that shitty restaurant!" Franks hands flew out in front of his body in a defiant and dismissive fashion.

"Besides, your boss is a fucking dick. You should give him the finger and make some real cheddar with me."

"Look, man, I got no problem with you doing this cat burglar shit..." Sam shook his head in a disapproving fashion slightly, "...but that's not my style."

"Not your Style? So being broke and sleeping on a couch in your tiny ass apartment is some fashion statement?" Retaliated Frank. "I've seen your refrigerator man; you got ketchup, beer and leftover Ramen noodles. Your job barely pays enough for the rent on your place. I am talking about making twenty grand in a single night."

Sam's' head snapped up, and his eyes drilled into Franks. He could barely believe what he heard, "Twenty grand...? No fucking way. What are you robbing? A bank?"

There is no way that anybody Sam knew was making that kind of cash. Especially not in a single day. Frank was right. It was more than Sam was making for an entire year's worth of work. He was only pulling in $18,000 a year washing dishes. Frank was also spot on about his boss. He was a dick. Nevertheless, Sam was always one to play devil's advocate.

"Who is going to pay us ten grand a piece to steal some shit when they could just do it themselves? What's the catch?" Sam questioned.

Frank grinned because he knew how Sam worked. He could tell that Sam was considering it and just needed a little push in the right direction. He loved his friend to death, but he knew Sam was a bit sheepish and just needed a good shepherd for tough decisions like these.

That is when Frank pulled out the ace stashed up his

sleeve, "Try 20 grand… a piece. The job pays $40,000 and there ain't no catch. This place doesn't even have a security system."

The smile on Frank's face grew from ear to ear. Tickled about the details of it, Frank could have sold it to anybody. He went on to talk about it a bit more, "Look bro we slip in and slip out. Only a couple of people even knows this thing is there. It will be weeks before they even know its missing. Piece-o-cake."

"What thing?" Sam asked with intrigue. "What are we stealing some old ass car or something?"

"Listen to this…it's a flower," Frank said with a look on his face expressing how lame and ridiculous the concept of stealing a flower was.

It didn't matter to him what they would be stealing; money was money. "I guess my boss is some flower nut or something. He is old; maybe flowers are his thing."

Too good to be true was the first thought that crossed Sam's mind. Nothing in life is ever that easy. However, the thought of easy money tends to wash out the reality of that saying. Especially when you are talking about easy money to a person who is broke and eating leftover ramen. No matter how hard he worked at his job, there was no way he was going to make that kind of money. Also, this was nontaxable and untraceable. Sam heard multiple stories from Frank about how easy it all was. He would slip in and swipe something, and that was that.

Frank never made mention about any encounters with the police or even security guards for that matter. He always dressed nice, drove a nice car and lived in a great apartment uptown. His parents were dirt poor, and there was no way Frank was getting this kind of cash from them. He couldn't be selling drugs. Frank detested the thought of drugs. All his money he had must have been coming from his rather questionable "night job."

The thought of getting caught never left Sam's mind. He never knew anyone that went to prison, but he heard enough folklore and urban legends about prison life to want to avoid going there. He did not intend to become a career thief, but he was tired of his dietary options and shitty boss. This heist needed to be a one-time thing. Slip in and slip out. Get paid and hang it up forever.

"I'm in. But just this once. When and where?" He said, feeling like he just sold his soul to the devil.

The feeling of uneasiness came over him as soon as the words left his mouth. What did he get himself into? Stealing was the last thing he thought he would be doing with his evening. He was on the schedule to work tonight. What was he going to tell his boss? How was he going to get that asshole to let him off this evening with such short notice? What was he supposed to wear? Did he need special tools? So many questions and so many details. It was going to be a long evening.

Chapter 6: The Smell of…

Several hours later Sam faced the point of no return. Frank said to meet at 8:30 pm. It was thirty minutes after his shift started at the restaurant. It was 8 o'clock. If he owned a phone, it would start blowing up any minute now with an asshole on the other end screaming at him and threatening his job. He needed to get his mind in the right place. One big payday. Twenty grand in a single evening. Fuck his boss. Fuck being broke. "Let's do this!" he thought to himself.

A half hour later, he was at the spot where Frank said to meet him. It was a surprisingly public place, the courtyard of a major shopping pavilion. There were tons of lights and people walking around. It was Friday night. Things were in full tilt. This spot was always busy. It was right in the heart of the city. Sam kept reminding himself to keep cool. He was constantly looking over his shoulder at the two cops hired as security at this courtyard. They were unaware why he was here. He was also overly concerned about seeing a fellow co-worker. He felt as though he were going to get into some serious trouble for ditching work. Then he realized that anyone that would recognize him was at work, probably trying to cover for him not being there. When it all came down to it, Sam had yet to commit a crime that he was aware of, but that did not stop him from feeling as if he was seconds away from being busted.

Only a few minutes had passed before Frank showed up. He crept up behind Sam without him noticing, nudged him in the shoulder and with a very authoritative voice said, "What are you doing here son!"

Sam flinched hard and spun around to see his accuser, heart pounding and full of adrenaline already. A wave of relief came over him as though he just got a shot of morphine when he saw that there was no threat and that it was in fact just his money-obsessed, retard of a best friend.

Frank laughed aloud and pointed at Sam, "You were scared out of your mind! That was the funniest shit I've seen all day!"

Sam shoved Frank slightly with the charge of "Asshole!"

Frank did not appear dressed for a caper. He was dressed in the same gear he was wearing earlier today, red shorts and a long white T-shirt, except a backpack that looked almost empty. He was dressed the complete opposite of how Sam dressed. He was wearing black shorts and shoes, a white T-shirt and a black long sleeve shirt tied around his waist. He was wearing a backpack as well, but it was full of gloves, a ski mask, a bit of rope, some pliers and wire cutters. When questioned by Frank about what was in the backpack, he was a bit reluctant to say. He informed Frank that he didn't know what he needed to bring…so he came prepared. He packed the type of stuff you see thieves wearing in the movies. He even brought a pair of black pants in there in case his shorts showed off too much of his identity. Once again, Frank chuckled in his normal fashion and called Sam a fool.

"Ain't nobody gonna see us where we're going," Frank said to Sam as they walked.

Turning into an alley next to the pavilion, Frank asked to see Sam's bag. Sam, of course, forked it over, and Frank threw it into a dumpster.

"You don't need all that; we'll pick it up on the way back." Sam stopped for a moment as if he was ready to say something but then just sighed and followed suit with Frank.

After a few blocks of turns and alleys, they came to a manhole cover. There was nothing special about this manhole cover. It was just there in the middle of the alley. The words "City Sewer" were stamped into the metal. Nothing more. There was nothing special about the alley either. No banks close by and no art museums. In fact, there wasn't even a greenhouse within a few miles of this alley. Frank reached into his backpack, pulled out a tiny little crowbar, and proceeded to pop the manhole cover from the top of the manhole.

Moments later, they managed to remove the cover from the hole. The smell that wafted out of the black hole was putrid. It smelled like a combination of shit, and week-old raw hamburger that was left in the car on a summer day, with just a twinge of sulfur to add some flavor. Sam and Frank gagged for a second.

"We've got to go down there?" Sam questioned. "God, it smells so bad!"

"It smells like money to me," Frank replied, "let's get going."

With an "ugh" and a single shake of the head, Sam followed Frank down the hole. It was a narrow fit. Just barely enough for his shoulders to get through. The trip down seemed cramped as well. All of the comic books and movies got it wrong. There was no massive substructure below the city streets. No long large tunnels with pristine walkways on either side of the crystal clean water. Instead, it was a very dark claustrophobic space, at least here it was.

The most you could do was crouch in the knee-deep water. Moreover, the water was anything but clean. It smelled horrible and felt even worse. As soon as Sam set foot into the ghastly sludge running through the pipes, he could swear he felt a turd brush against his leg. In this dark, dank tunnel it could have been any number of things.

To top it all off, Frank handed Sam a flashlight. The instant he flipped the switch he saw that the walls were crawling with roaches. Roaches by the thousands. They didn't seem to scatter like roaches in his apartment. The chances are that these roaches have never seen a human and were completely unbothered by their presence. "What the FUCK! Dude, we gotta move man!" Sam shouted to Frank.

They began to push forward through the ever so cramped space, wading and swatting the fallen roaches from their neck and hair as they trekked through the long maze of tunnels.

After what felt like an eternity in this dark Hell of a rank, roach infested nothingness Sam shouted, "HOW MUCH FURTHER?!"

Frank replied, "Should only be about fifty or sixty more feet and it'll open up, we'll check the map there."

Frank was right on the money. After about fifty feet the treacherous tube of crawling walls and soupy sludge opened up into a cross pipe. One with much more space but just as gross. Sam continued to brush the roaches from his body, and as he shined the flashlight down on himself, he became even more disgusted.

It appeared as though half the stuff in the sewer they just waded through was still clinging to his clothes. Dozens of unidentifiable stains were dripping and oozing down his shorts and onto his legs. A mysterious slimy substance made its way into his shoe causing his toes to slip and slide against each other inside of his overly saturated sock. It was far worse than he predicted the night would be.

"How much further does it say on the map?" Sam asked.

"About a quarter mile that way down this pipe and we will come to a door. What we are looking for will be on the other side."

Frank placed the laminated map back into his pack and slung it over his shoulder. He could see the frustration on Sam's face.

He smiled and said "Easy money, man. After this, you can take a long shower and tomorrow when we get paid; we can go shopping. All this will just be a memory, and you'll be a lot wealthier."

Frank's reassurances were weak at best. Sam was completely grossed out. If there were not such a large payday on the line, he would have turned back by now. However, a small part of him was enjoying the adventure. Even as a little kid he would look down into storm drains and wonder what lay hidden below the streets. This was much worse than anything he ever dreamed about but still slightly intriguing to the kid in him. With one final flinch and a rapid brush of a roach crawling up his arm, they carried on.

The final part of the journey was far less difficult than the first part. The water was only ankle deep; there seemed to be a lot less crap in it. There was still just as many roaches and bugs, but since the tunnel was twice the height of Frank and Sam and wide enough to get two cars through, they did not seem to bother the duo. As they approached the end of the tunnel, the sound of rushing water filled the air.

"Must be a drop off up ahead," Frank said in a slightly louder voice. He raised his voice to compete with the waterfall's overpowering sound.

"Boy, that rope sure would've come in real handy right about now huh...?" Frank could almost taste the sarcasm coming from Sam.

They got to the edge of the pipe and stopped to look at what lay beyond the end of the pipe. Their flashlights could barely illuminate the cavernous room that was in before them. One thing was apparent, though, it was about twenty feet down to the bottom of the waterfall, and there was no way to tell how deep the water was.

"What now?" Sam asked.

Frank's only reply was a grin. He took his pack from his back and reached inside. He pulled out several plastic sticks, each about a foot long.

He handed his pack to Sam and said, "Hold this."

He cracked and shook each of the sticks one by one, and they began to glow in a range of colors. Some were blue, some were yellow, and others were green. He drew back and tossed them out into the huge cavernous space. All but one. It was only a few seconds before the light revealed a large part of the room to them. It was a truly massive space. From what they could see, it was the size of a football stadium. The water seemed to cover most of it; but on the opposite side, there was a large set of boulders sitting on top of space not submerged by the water. Each boulder was as big as a car or bigger. This room was completely out of place. Rooms of this size did not belong in the sewer.

Frank grabbed one of the pipes that were running along the wall for support and leaned out over the waterfall. He dropped his remaining glow stick over the edge so that it fell into the pool of water below. It sunk further and further. It almost went out of site. Only a small glow remained by the time it settled to the bottom of the pool.

"Looks deep enough to me," Frank said as he looked back at Sam.

With the shit-eating grin Frank was so famous for, he let go of the pipe that was supporting his weight and leaped from the edge of the waterfall. On the way down he shouted, "Hope you can swim!" and then plunged into the pool head first.

Sam held his breath, anxiously waiting for him to resurface. It only took about five seconds for him to come up for air. Those five seconds might as well have been five minutes in Sam's book.

"Come on down; it's plenty deep. You'll be okay!"

Sam could barely hear Frank over the rush of the waterfall and the crash of the water hitting the pool. Suddenly he realized he was in the same position as earlier today on the roof. Here was this massive jump sitting before him. He was too far in to back out, and now his pride was on the line (not to mention a massive payday.) His best friend already took the plunge and now it was his turn.

"I can't bitch out on this one," he told himself.

He quit his job for this adventure, committed himself to crawling through the muck and bug infested pipes. He even sacrificed his morals. What was a little jump? He backed up about ten feet, slung Franks bag on his back and assumed a runner's stance.

"SHIT! SHIT! SHIT! AAARRRRRRGGGHHHHH!!!" He screamed as he bolted out in a dead sprint for the edge of the tunnel and jumped out into almost pure darkness.

The glow sticks offered little illumination from this height. He couldn't tell how long it would take to hit the water or how deep it was. What if he hit a hidden pipe or something that Frank missed? Oh well, too late to worry about that now. Funny thing about flying through the dark, you always hit after you think you should. With a thunderous splash, Sam crashed into the pool below. Nose pinched, and feet pointed. As he shot under the water, something strange happened. Time rather slowed down a bit, at least for Sam it did. He felt a strange warmth and calmness flow over his body. It was as if he was supposed to be there. He was not afraid of what may be hidden under the water or what was going to happen next. He just calmed down.

Amid all the calmness, he heard a voice from deep inside. It was his voice, but it was not him talking.

The voice said "It's OK. Just let it happen and it will all be OK. You are here for a reason."

Even the voice was soothing. There was absolutely no reason to doubt the voice in his head. It was not his voice, but it was offering words of encouragement. He never felt so confident about his current situation. He wasn't worried about the sludge that covered him. The bugs that were still crawling around in his shirt didn't seem to worry him. His heart was racing but not from fear. He was just confident and peaceful. It was the best he felt in years.

As he calmly came up and broke the surface of the water, he took in a deep breath and wiped the water from his eyes, he looked around the dimly lit room. He surveyed across the top of the water looking for Frank, but Frank was nowhere to be found. Suddenly he noticed the glow from the stick that was at the bottom of the pool was growing brighter and closer. Seconds later

Frank Surfaced with the glow stick in his hand and said, "Couldn't leave this behind."

In his newly calmed state, Sam said, "Thanks, Man. That was epic. I needed that."

"Of course man, I needed a homie on this with me," Frank said in the most macho way possible considering the two were treading water in a sewer while sharing a bro moment.

As many men trying to be macho do, he followed up with "Now stop being such a fag and let's get out of this nasty water."

The pair swam across the massive room to the only spot that did not have water. It was a small landing about the size of a city intersection. There was very little detail. The walls seemed to be formed concrete with very little texture to them at all. On the far side of this landing was the pile of large boulders that they saw earlier. Now they could get a better sense of the layout. The boulders were randomly stacked on either side of a massive door. At least, they assumed it was a door.

It was about twenty feet high and split from top to bottom down the center. A giant slab of concrete crossed the door horizontally. The entire structure was concrete, but it did not look like the formed concrete from the surrounding walls. This concrete appeared to be much older. It was gritty and dark; there was a moldy mossy substance growing out from the center crack between the two doors. Scrolled across the barricade were symbols that Sam and Frank couldn't identify.

They looked like runes, but neither of them knew what runes looked like exactly, so it was just shy of an educated guess. Frank raised the glow stick above his head to get a better look.

"What do you think that shit says?" he asked.

"Just a guess...Stay the fuck out," Sam answered in a very monotone manner that could have been witty if he were not so serious about what he said.

He then asked, "Is this the door you were talking about?"

"Yep...I don't see any other doors...do you?" Frank replied.

"What about that one?" Sam pointed to a barely visible door stashed away behind the boulders.

It was a small black door with no handle, only hinges. There was no way of telling what was on the other side of this door. The light did not even shine from underneath it. Frank walked over to the door with a glow stick in hand. He surveyed it for only a moment and then turned and walked back to the massively ominous door made of concrete.

"Nope...Boss said it was the big door."

"Did he mention how to get in this big ass door?" Sam

questioned again.

"Yep...Let me see that pack."

Frank grabbed the bag from Sam's hand and started rummaging through it. Sam turned around and stepped a few feet away while pulling his pack of thoroughly drenched smokes from his shorts pocket. Not even one survived. Still he pulled one out. He then started trying to get his lighter to work. It took some blowing and quite a few strikes, but he finally got it going.

He became so relaxed at this point that there was no stress about his cigarette being wet. He simply lit the lighter and started rotating the smoke over it to dry it out. A couple of minutes passed and he felt confident that it would light.

Sam placed the butt between his lips and set fire to the tip. It was a pathetic struggle, but the fire-dried cigarette took a spark and rushed the nicotine fix to his lungs. It tasted like complete shit, but it did the trick. Sam noticed that Frank was humming a tune in the background. It was more like a failed attempt at beatboxing the 'Mission Impossible' theme, but considering the situation, it seemed appropriate.

He paid no attention to his partner in crime for the past several minutes. He was so focused on lighting his cigarette that Frank's doings now were of no real concern to him. Still, he wondered what was going on.

Frank spoke up "Yo, lemme see that lighter."

Sam turned to hand the lighter to Frank and was caught totally off guard by what he saw. Frank managed to tape three sticks of dynamite to the door. Sam had never seen real dynamite before, but the black stencil on the side of the sticks that said "DYNAMITE" was a dead giveaway. Though unprepared for this, he remained eerily calm. Since his dip in the pool, nothing seemed to faze him.

"That is totally gonna wake up the neighbors, man," He said. "Where the fuck did you get dynamite?"

"My boss is the shit. He said we were going to need it." *clearly knew where the flower is*

Frank's face was lit up like a Christmas tree. He dreamed of a moment like this all his life. It's not every day that a kid from the city gets to blow stuff up with dynamite in the sewers of a major metropolis. He flicked the still damp lighter a couple of times until it caught flame. With absolutely no hesitation, he lit the fuse attached to the dynamite. By movie standards, the fuse was quite long, about 8 inches. However, this wasn't a movie, and the sparkling fuse rushed towards the stick way faster than he anticipated. Both of them scrambled as fast as they could and just barely made it behind one of the boulders before the explosion.

What an explosion it was. Rubble and debris went flying everywhere. The sound reverberated off the walls of the underground enclosure. The fuse burned so fast there was no time to cover their ears before the blast. They could hear pieces of rock landing in the water faintly over the piercing ring that echoed in their eardrums. As they stood up to survey the damage, nothing was even visible. The smoke that filled the air was thick and the glow from Frank's stick didn't offer adequate light to pierce through it. Sam waved his hand in front of his face and coughed slightly.

He looked down and saw his cigarette still lit on the ground, "Dope," he said as he reached over and picked it up and took a draw.

Frank wasted no time. He darted around the protection of the boulder back towards the door eager to see the fruits of his explosive labor. Upon reaching the door, nothing but disappointment came from his lips.

"Man... damn!" He said, "This should have made a way bigger hole than this!"

The dynamite managed to blow a small wedge out of the door. It was about three feet high, and the base of the wedge was about two and a half feet across. Sam placed his hand on the door.

As he leaned into the newly formed hole just a bit, he said, "Well, at least, we can get in."

Without hesitation, he crouched down and wormed his way through the small space. The door must have been at least two feet thick and was completely solid. The hole blown in it was slightly smaller on the other side. Once he crawled through Sam stood up into the vastly dark room. He could smell the burnt gunpowder and dust from the concrete. At first, the odors seemed to overpower his nose. As he walked further into the black, he could smell fresh air like he was in a forest. There was a musk to it, a completely different smell than the sewer he was just standing in. The air was about 10 degrees cooler and not as humid.

Frank made his way into the room with a glow stick in hand and brought with him light. The room was a giant dome. The walls appeared made of solid rock. Not jagged or rough, but rather polished. In fact, it was smooth as glass. The roof was about fifty feet high at its apex. The room itself was half of a perfect sphere, occupied by nothing more than a box made of the same polished stone in the very center.

As the two of them began to move towards the box, they noticed the moss underfoot. As they got even closer to it, they could see that vines were growing out from around the box. Sam found this to be very strange because there was no water and no sunlight in this room. Except for the box, the moss, and the vines, there was nothing else in the room.

"Strange place to keep a flower, Frank," Sam said in a very low tone.

His head was on a swivel trying to take it all in. Frank said nothing. His head was on a similar swivel. They were both in awe of where they were. As they approached the box, they could see similar writing to that which was on the giant door. It might as well have been written in Chinese. Neither Frank nor Sam had a clue what it said.

"What do you think this says?" Frank questioned.

"I know what it says...Don't open this fucking box," Sam replied as he continued to look around

The one thing Frank could identify was the handprint on the box's lid. He pulled the glow stick ever so close to it. The handprint appeared remarkably detailed. It was as if someone spent a great deal of time carving each line of his or her hand into the well-polished rock lid. The handprint was devoid of any dust or dirt, and there were no markings except a single black dot in the center of the palm.

Frank placed his hand into the impression but it was a poor fit. His hand was just a bit too large, and his fingers were too long. There was a very bizarre sensation to it. With the room being so cool, Frank fully expected the stone to feel the same; yet, it was strangely warm. It felt like touching another person's hand. It was creepy, to say the least.

"What the...hey man, check this shit out," he called out.

Sam walked over the box and stood beside Frank.

"Look at that detail. It's amazing," Sam said as he leaned in closer to get a better look.
"It feels so freaky, put your hand in there. It's warm." Frank said.

Sam placed his hand into the print and surprisingly, it felt like his own. Everything lined up perfectly. Every line, every crease, and fold were an exact match. Strangely, it was an exact match to his hand print.

"Weird," he said in as calm a voice as possible.

He could feel the warmth that Frank was talking about. There was a slight tingle, similar to the feel of tiger balm- just a bit more intense. Then the print began to glow beneath his hand. He quickly snatched his hand away. He felt almost blinded by the bright white-hot light that came from the handprint. They both put their hands in front of their eyes trying to shield themselves from the shocking white light.

As quickly as it began, it ended.

"What the FUCK did you do, Sam?" Wiping his eyes as though he just stepped out of the dark and into the sunlight.

Frank staggered a bit, "I can't see shit!"

Suddenly the box began to make a grinding noise. Sam managed to get just enough of his sight back to see that the lid was sliding off the top of the box. Completely bewildered, he continued to wipe his eyes just a bit, hoping to clear up his vision and get readjusted to the dark. As the box opened further and further, he noticed a slight glow coming from down inside. The lid made a thud as it dropped off the edge of the box and one side landed on the ground. Sam and Frank both peered into the box and saw something truly beautiful and utterly unique. Inside of this box was a solid white glowing flower.

It stood about a foot tall with twelve triangular shaped petals on it. The center was large and round like a DVD, only bulbous instead of flat. The stem was bleached white, with no leaves. The roots at the base were visible above the surface, but only just. The pair stood in awe for a moment. They were trying to get a handle on what they just experienced. Strange writing and glowing handprints in stone boxes? Self-moving heavy lids? A glowing flower growing in the middle of a dark underground dome? It all seemed a bit surreal, like a fantasy novel; but, it was all too real.

Frank even questioned it aloud to make sure, "Are we dreaming? I mean...Are we seeing this? We aren't in the matrix or no shit like that, are we?"

"Nope...That's a real glowing flower in that box. Now I get why we are making so much money on this."

Sam never even blinked. Both he and Frank kept their eyes on the flower the whole time.

"So... How do we get this thing out of here without killing it?" Sam asked.

He knew nothing about flowers, but he did know enough to know that they were fragile and delicate.

"Boss said to grab it at the base and pull it out of the ground," Frank said, still staring at it.

"Just pull it out? Just like that?" Sam asked.

"Yup. Just pull it out."

"Okay, Captain Cat Burglar...get to pulling," Sam broke his attention away from the flower long enough to give Frank a bit of hell.

Frank gave Sam the finger and leaned into the box. He was slightly hesitant on wrapping his hand around the base of the flower due to its mystical appearance. He closed his eyes, squinted and snapped his hand onto the flower's stalk. He gave the flower a solid tug to pull it from the ground. Nothing happened.

"Damn...this thing is in there pretty solid," he said.

Again, he gave it a solid tug using twice the force he did before. Nothing happened. Frank then wrapped both hands onto the base and pulled with all of his might. He let out a mighty scream in an attempt to get every bit of strength he could, and still, nothing happened. The flower did not budge. In fact, it did not shake, wiggle, or move even the slightest bit. It was as though the flower were made of stone as well.

"I swear to God! To be such a badass, you sure are a pussy," Sam said making fun of Frank.

"You think it's so easy...you do it," Frank quickly replied in a very "kiss-my-ass" tone.

Sam kicked his head back slightly in agreement and leaned into the box. Before he could get his hand on the base of the flower, they heard a small noise and a voice in the large room they just came through to get here. They looked at each other, and their hearts began to race. Was it a security guard? Maybe it was just city workers checking out the sound from the explosion? Could it be the cops way down here?

"We've got to get out of here," Frank whispered to Sam.

"How? There are no other doors," Sam replied.

"We gotta go out the way we came," said Frank.

"Oh, that's smart! Go toward the voices that could be cops! Brilliant!" Sam rattled.

They began to see faint traces of flashlights searching around. From the number of beams, there were several people on the other side of that gigantic concrete door.

"I got an idea," Frank whispered, "I still have a stick of dynamite left..."

Sam shot a what the fuck look at Frank. The kind of look that questioned his mode of thinking for saving a stick of dynamite.

"So I like to blow shit up, get over it! We could light it, throw it out the door, wait till it blows and make a run for it unless you got a better idea," Frank said.

Sam pondered his options for all of about a quarter of a second.

"Shit," he said as he dropped his head a bit. He looked back up at Frank and asked: "What about the flower?"

"We'll grab it and take it with us. If we make it, at least, we'll get paid."

It sounded like a pretty solid idea to Sam. He wasted no time reaching in and grabbing the flower at the base. He gave it the slightest tug, and it slipped right out of the ground. Sam held the flower in front of him and looked at it trying to figure why Frank was not able to pull it out of the ground. Given the situation, he quickly dismissed it as Frank playing a joke on him. While he was holding it, the glow slowly began to fade from it. It only took it a few seconds until the glow was all but gone.

He looked up, and Frank already began moving towards the door. Sam snapped to his feet and scrambled to catch up with him. Taking a position beside the hole they created earlier, Frank reached into the backpack and pulled out the last stick of dynamite. He held his hand out to Sam and began flipping his fingers in a request for Sam's lighter once again.

"The instant this thing blows, we make a run for it. Don't hesitate. Got me?" Frank snapped the order to Sam in the quietest voice possible.

Sam simply nodded his head and hoped that this would work. He was not looking forward to this plan. But, there was no other choice. At least, this line of thought gave them a chance of escape, which was more than they had if they stayed in this room.

Frank lit the fuse and waited for it to get close to the stick before tossing it. Once it flew out the door, the duo covered their ears and leaned away from the hole. It was only a split second later that the explosion came. Sam and Frank scrambled out the door fully expecting everyone out there to be disoriented; however, it was quite the opposite. Where they expected four or five people, there were 30 heavily armed soldiers in full tactical gear. They anticipated the dynamite would, at least, create a distraction; the soldiers were well protected behind the safety of a wall of riot shields.

They stopped dead in their tracks. Frank dropped his bag and raised his hands to the sky. Sam attempted to drop the flower, but he could not get his hand to let go of it. He raised his hands and said to Frank

"We are so fucked."

Chapter 7: The First Petal

"Now I am become Death. The destroyer of worlds."
-The Bhagavad Gita-

Blinded by the mass of light beams shining on their faces from the multitude of flashlights, Sam and Frank stood nervously surrounded by what looked to be about 30 heavily armed soldiers. There was no sound except for a single voice. Though they could not tell which of the soldiers it was coming from.

"Yes sir, we've got them," the soldiers voice said.

There was no audible reply to the soldier's remarks. It was as if they were listening to one side of a phone conversation.

He continued, "Just two. What are your orders?"

There was an eerie silence that came after that. The only thing that could they could hear was the waterfall in the distance behind the soldiers.

Then that silence was broken yet again by the soldier's voice. "Yes sir."

A single soldier stepped through the wall of riot shields. It was impossible to make out his face with all the lights behind him. He reached to his hip, pulled out a pistol and shot both Frank and Sam in the head one time each. There could not have been a more effortless task. There was no hesitation. He did not even think about it. He just shot them.

Frank and Sam fell dead to the ground like rag dolls. Their blood splattered on the massive concrete door they emerged from. As they lay on the ground, the blood from their heads poured out into immense puddles beneath them. It began to soak into their clothes, as they lay lifeless. Eventually, Sam's pool of blood made it to the white flower that was still locked tightly in his hand. It too became soaked with his blood.

The soldier again called for orders. The reply he got was to get the flower, dispose of the bodies and return topside for debriefing. The soldier relayed the orders to his men. As he walked over to Sam's body and reached down to grab the flower he noticed Sam's hand twitching. The soldier shrugged it off thinking it was probably the remaining impulses of life and electricity leaving the body. He tried to take the flower from his lifeless hand but was unsuccessful. Even though he was dead, Sam's grip was as rigid as ever.

Sam's body began to move just a bit more. First a twitch of the leg. Then, a twitch of the arm. The soldier looked directly at the flower. The once pristine white flower became so soaked in Sam's blood that it became a dark red. It was as if it drank the blood from the ground like water. There was not a single spot of white left on it.

The soldier stood up and slowly started backing away from the body on the ground.

Sam was swiftly becoming more animated. As he miraculously sprung back to life, he stood up and wobbled a bit. His head was down as he caught his balance and stopped moving completely. At that moment, a single petal of the flower turned to black ash as though it was set on fire; only there was no fire. The petal simply wilted and fell from the flower in the form of black dust.

The soldier quickly retreated behind the wall of riot shields and shouted to the other soldiers to "OPEN FIRE!"

The clicking and clacking of weapons gave way to a barrage of muzzle flashes and ear-piercing gunfire. Hundreds of rounds were fired at Sam's newly reanimated body. Soldiers emptied entire cartridges of bullets. And when the firing stopped, Sam was still standing. Not a single bullet hit him. The red hot bullets all stopped less than an inch from his body. All the soldiers could see was the silhouette of Sam's body covered in bullets. They just stopped, frozen in time.

Only a second or two went by before the soldiers began to shuffle back a step or two. No one had ever seen anything like that. Half of the soldiers there were battle-hardened in Iraq and Afghanistan. Half of those had taken a bullet or seen their buddies die or lose a limb to IEDs. But none of them ever witnessed something like this.

Sam took in a very deep breath. On the inhale his head raised up and dropped backward as though there were no muscles in his neck. He exhaled, and the bullets that stopped right in front of him retreated by about a foot. Once again, he took in a deep breath. In between the inhale and exhale Sam's head snapped to an upright position. His eyes jumped open in a moment of complete focus. They were glowing white just like the flower while it was still in the box. Sam's pupils completely disappeared.

He shouted at the top of his lungs. It was so loud that the walls and floor of the landing began to vibrate. The water that came up to the surface of the landing retreated about two feet and started to ripple out and create waves. The roar shot across the room so violently that it disrupted the flow of the waterfall that Sam and Frank jumped from only minutes ago.

All of the soldiers grabbed their ears trying to keep their ear drums from bursting as they stumbled back from the force of the sound coming from Sam. The volume on his scream quickly tapered down and stopped. The echo continued for just a moment. Then the room once again became silent. Awe and disbelief were running rampant among the soldiers. What they just experienced was so unreal. But nothing could have prepared them for what happened next.

Sam took a slight step back with his left foot as if he

were adjusting his stance for better balance. He crossed his forearms in front of his face and took in another deep breath. With a second thunderous scream, he uncrossed his arms and flung them backward with such a tremendous amount of force that it sent the bullets that were still hovering in front of him back to where they came at twice the speed. Those without riot shields were torn to shreds. Limbs, blood and chunks of flesh scattered across the landing like a thick beef stew thrown from a huge pot. Twelve of the men died instantly.

Many others were left screaming and crying on the ground, writhing in pain and pools of their blood. Some bled out seconds later. A few of those that were protected by the riot shields were stunned...shell shocked. Not physically injured, just unable to process the situation at hand. Their buddies were decimated by a guy that came back to life and threw their bullets back at them.

Three of the nine men left standing made a dash for the small black door that they came in. Sam was quick. He had anticipated an attempt to flee and solved the problem. With a quick skip step to his right side, he kicked a car-sized boulder and forced it to slide towards the door, not only to block their escape but to crush and kill the three soldiers in the process. The boulder made a thunderous grinding sound as it slid across the floor.

One of the remaining six began firing on Sam with his pistol. One shot made a connection with his left shoulder, and another hit his right forearm. Neither of the two bullets broke the skin. Sam's attention snapped to the soldier that was taking pot shots at him. Moving so fast that he left streaks behind him, Sam charged towards the soldier and stopped mere inches from him. The soldier was hit by a blast of wind so strong that it rocked his balance a bit.

This soldier was blank with fear. He was standing face to face with the scariest thing he had ever seen. A man that moved faster than he could see. A man that bullets didn't seem to faze. A man that was nothing like a man at all. Sam leaned in ever so slightly and growled as the soldier stumbled backward in fear. Unable to cope and unable to think of anything else but his own life the soldier raised his pistol to shoot again. He fired off two shots. Sam dodged them both effortlessly and grabbed the soldier's wrist.

With the ferocity of a starving lion, he ripped the man's arm from his body just below the shoulder. There was a grotesque sound of bone cracking and tendon snapping and a massive splatter of blood that sprayed the soldiers beside him. With a swift pirouette, Sam spun around and smacked the soldier with his severed arm. It was as if he were hitting a home run with a baseball bat. The soldier rocketed across the massive room slamming into the wall only feet from the waterfall. Immediately after hitting the soldier Sam sped after him.

Running across the water like a hovercraft and up the wall like a lizard to meet the soldier when he impacted, standing straight up on the wall as though it were the floor, Sam reared his fist back and smashed the soldiers head before gravity could take hold and pull him to the water that was about fifteen feet below. The punch was swift and devastating. Sam's fist traveled all the way through the soldier's Kevlar helmet and into the wall creating a crater in the brick and mortar. The soldiers body separated from his now pulverized head at the neck and splashed down into the water below.

The five remaining soldiers quickly split up and headed for cover behind the massive boulders that surrounded the large concrete door. In rapid and random patterns, they started firing rounds at the beast of a man that Sam changed into. A flurry of those bullets pelted his skin creating little ripples as they made contact. None of them made it below the surface and into his body. Sam raised his hands and forearms in front of his face and turned his head to the side as though he were being splashed in the face with water.

Annoyed once again he sped into action, running parallel to the pool of water along the wall. Shards of brick and bits of concrete were flying off the wall behind him along with a dust trail. As he traveled, one of the soldiers fired a grenade from the launcher mounted to the bottom of his gun at him. Without hesitation, Sam stopped dead in his tracks and caught the grenade with one hand like a baseball. He crushed it in his hand and caused it to detonate. The explosion was massive and blew pieces from the wall in football sized chunks that rained down into the water. The entire area around him became covered in dust and smoke so thick that no one could see if the shot was effective.

Sam exploded from the smoke flying head first like a rocket at the dispersed band of horrified soldiers. Smashing into the ground in front of them, the force of his impact rippled across the small landing, breaking apart the concrete as it traveled away from him. He let out another furious scream. Gripped by fear, the soldiers did the only thing their training would allow them to do; they opened fire again.

This time, the bullets didn't even get close to Sam. They simply veered off course feet before they got to him. It was as if his will extended beyond his body and told the bullets where to go. The soldiers didn't stand a chance. Sam took one step forward and then another. Midway through the third step he exploded into a sprint so fast that the soldiers lost sight of him. All they could see were the bits of concrete flying up in the wake of his movement.

As if by magic he appeared in front of the first two soldiers with his hands around their necks. Sam squeezed his hands and pulled out their throats as easily as a person gripping a handle to a cabinet door and pulling it open. Dropping the fistfuls of destroyed tissue and muscle he took hold of the bodies by grabbing a hold of their rib cages and with a quick spin, sent them flying through the air towards two of the remaining three soldiers.

One body landed on the boulder they were using for cover. Blood spattered from the remnants of the throat onto their face. The other landed only a few feet behind them.

With blood all over his face, one of the two remaining soldiers kept saying "this shit ain't real man."

He repeated it over and over and over like some horrified mantra. Staring at the body that lay on the rock in front of him, he didn't notice that Sam zipped up behind him. Sam placed his hand on the back of his head and smashed it into the boulder. Caught completely off guard, the soldier next to him spun and began firing on Sam at point blank range. Even this close the ridiculous little bullets had no effect. Grabbing the fully automatic rifle by the barrel, Sam tore it from his hands. Raising the gun back over his shoulder, he brought it down to the soldier as if he were swinging a machete, embedding it into the man's skull.

From thirty to one. As the blood of twenty-nine of his companions spilled into the massive pool of water that was beginning to turn red, the last soldier cowered behind a rock. Deep in prayer and shaking violently, he did not raise his weapon. He simply buried his forehead into the back side of his thumbs, hands clasped so tightly that his knuckles were white. He sat and prayed. He prayed that this beast would not take him. He prayed that he would get to see his family again. He thought of nothing but his wife and two children.

Sam landed on the boulder he was hiding behind. He would not move. He continued to pray. Sam shouted at him like a wild beast claiming dominion over his territory. The soldier clenched his eyes shut tighter and fought back the tears. He was not afraid of his death. It was the thought of leaving his children without their father and the pain it would bring to his wife that scared him. This monster was simply the means to that end. Sam reached down and grabbed the back of the soldier's body armor and lifted him off the ground. The soldier struggled for a moment. He accepted his fate and was not struggling with fright or fear but more from discomfort.

Dragging him like a child dragging a teddy bear, Sam hopped from the top of the boulder to the ground. Turning his gaze toward the ceiling, he crouched down somewhat and jumped upwards with rocket-like speed. As he reached the roof, he raised his fist and smashed through the brittle concrete. His punch was focused and powerful enough to break through the many layers of dirt rock and pipe that lay above the room. It was only a moment or so until a massive explosion of rock and dirt blew through the asphalt of the city street above.

Chunks of rock the size of furniture leaped from underneath the ground by the dozens. They flew some 30 feet into the air and crashed back down onto the ground, smashing into cars and through the windows of the shops that lined this street. People began screaming as they scattered like roaches. The sound of tires screeching and cars smashing into one another filled the air as they all suddenly stopped to avoid the concrete and asphalt chaos that was raining from the sky. Alarms were blaring from all of the parked cars that were crushed by the falling stone.

Chapter 8: ...And He Appeared Before the Masses

As quickly as the chaos caused fear, it began to cause curiosity. People perceived the immediate threat to be over, and their attention turned toward the explosion. Through the cloud of dust, they could barely see a silhouette still holding the soldier by the back of his body armor. The soldier had his hands clasped around Sam's fist as though he were futilely trying to break his grip. Though he could move, he was stuck. His legs squirmed and wiggled, but it was as though he became pinned down by the weight of a building.

Sam drew his other hand and forearm back over his opposite shoulder and waved it quite swiftly across his body. As he did so, a massive wind rushed out from him and cleared away the dust that was still lingering in the air. People were blown back a step or two as they covered their faces with the dust flying at them. As the wind passed and attention drew back towards Sam, there were gasps and screams. People could not believe what they were seeing. And rightly so.

Before them stood a man that just exploded from the ground. He was the man that forced the dust from around him with a mere gesture. But these were only minor things compared to what they saw.

In front of them was a man that was surrounded by an ominous red glow. The lustrous red light seemed to flicker from him on all sides. The glow was intense, but not bright. It radiated from him about five feet in all directions and performed like swirling the water in a bottle at the base and as a flame at the top. Little pieces of debris floated from the ground inside of the glow. He was truly a sight to behold, and it was only a matter of seconds before the cell phones came out and began to film him.

Sam hurled the soldier from his side. He slammed into the windshield of a car that stopped about 20 feet from the explosion. The man took a second to gather himself, realizing that his prayers had been answered. He also realized that his body armor saved him from any serious damage caused by slamming into the car's windshield. Luck favored the prepared.

Slowly he rolled off the hood of the sedan and painfully brought himself to his feet. He looked at Sam with a look that questioned: "What next?"

Swirling in the powerful red glow was the thing that killed twenty-nine of his buddies. Violently and viciously this monster annihilated seasoned warriors. Warriors that fought by his side in some of the most serious battles he experienced.

Warriors that were trained, heavily armed and well-guarded by shields and body armor. What would he do to these people? The shock of that thought overwhelmed and paralyzed him. He was barely able to cope with the horrific scene he just endured. The mere thought of seeing all of these innocent people die as well was too much. He just stared at Sam as he slumped down against the car he just smashed.

Just then Sam's eyes locked with the soldier. The glowing white gaze of his was mesmerizing. It burned deep into the soldier's soul. It was the kind of stare that showed utter dominance and control; powerful in will, confident and deadly. Without warning, a thought popped into the beaten soldier's head. Although it wasn't a thought in his voice, the thought was ferocious and intimidating. It growled as it spoke and reverberated through his mind, not allowing any other thoughts to pass. It was excruciatingly loud in nature, like standing next to a speaker at a concert.

"I will kill them all," the voice said.

The soldier felt incredibly nauseous as the piece of malicious verbiage echoed through his head. Then it clicked. The thought belonged to the monster, not him. That's why he wasn't moving or attacking. He was waiting. This monstrosity of a person wanted the people to run in fear. The soldier looked around to see everyone on the street mesmerized, much as he was. No one was moving, they all just stared in disbelief at this thing before them. The soldier looked back at Sam.

Suddenly the red glow surrounding him pulsed out a bit and began to change colors. From the reddish hue that it was, the pulse became more of gold and started to swirl faster.

Again the thought raced through the soldier's head, will kill them all."

Only, this time, it was far stronger and much louder. He no longer felt nausea as he did before. Instead, he was overcome by a sense of purpose. His adrenaline began to flow as he realized that the only way to protect these people from what was about to happen was to make them scared. To get them to put down their damn phones and run. He couldn't be scared anymore. He had only a moment to get them out of there. He needed to act; he had to do it right then before it was too late.

The soldier stood up and began running toward the people shouting and waving his arms, "RUN! GO! YOU GOTTA GO!!!"

Quickly the attentions of those staring at Sam were broken by the soldier screaming at them to run. First, it was only a few that paid attention and began to run, but within seconds, there was a full-scale panic as people fled from their cars and stores and started running away from the glowing man standing in the middle of the street.

The screams of men and women filled the air and overpowered the still chirping car alarms. The soldier ran with them for only a few feet before he looked back. He stopped running and turned back towards Sam. It was as though he was compelled to stay and see what happened next. He could hear the sound of helicopters and sirens coming towards them.

The police were unaware of what they were rushing into. If this monster treated them anything like he treated those men down in that hole, things were about to get bloody.

Like a beam of light from Heaven, a spotlight flashed down on Sam from the sky. It was a light from a police helicopter. An amplified voiced pierced through the air, shouting orders.

"Get down face first on the ground!" The police helicopter was barking. "Get down or we will open fire!" It shouted again.

Just then, the second beam of light burst from another police helicopter to further illuminate Sam.

"This is your final warning. Get down face first on the ground or we will be forced to shoot you."

From every direction dozens of police cars screeched onto the scene. Officers jumped out of their vehicles and took cover behind car doors and the bodies of their cruisers and S.U.V.'s. Several pulled up behind the soldier as well. Four police officers ran in front of the soldier and began rushing him out of the line of fire. With his respect for authority built into him from his training, he complied.

The chief for this group of officers was close to where

they had ushered him to, and he could hear the helicopter speaking with him over the radio

"What should we do sir?" the helicopter asked.

"I don't quite know what that thing is. Let's see if we can get his attention," the Chief said "Fire a warning shot."

"Copy that," replied the chopper.

There was a loud crack that echoed against the buildings as a spark flashed off the asphalt. Sam did not flinch. Slowly he turned his head to look up at the helicopter. It was a look of dismissal. It was a look that said "Shoot me...I dare you." His attention turned back to the soldier.

"I will kill them all," The soldier heard in his head again.

This time, it was so intense that he puked. Doubled over on his knees, the soldier struggled to gain control of his nausea.

Lifting himself back to his feet by using the side of a police car, he wiped the vomit from his lips and mumbled to himself, "Yeah, I get it. Kill them all."

Trying to shake his nausea, he struggled to put one foot in front of the other, as he made his way toward the police chief. Slowly at first, but then he began to run.

His sudden sprint drew the attention of the many officers close to the Chief. They quickly intercepted and pointed their weapons at him.

"Don't move!" they shouted.

The soldier stopped and threw his hands into the air.

"DON'T SHOOT HIM....DON'T SHOOT HIM!" He shouted at the top of his lungs, "IF YOU SHOOT HIM HE WILL KILL ALL OF YOU!!!"

Dismissing the soldier as some raving lunatic, the police chief sent the order to the helicopter.

"Take the shot."

"NOOOOOOOO!!!" Shouted the soldier.

There was another crack that echoed from the buildings. One of the police helicopters fired a single round at Sam. That round stopped inches from the side of his head. Still spinning in midair was a high caliber bullet hovering there, waiting to deal a death blow to Sam. If it had not stopped, it would have torn his head completely from his body. As he stood there, brooding, turning to look at the bullet, the glow around Sam began to pulse and turned from gold to a deep dark purple and then sucked inward and swiftly disappeared. The bullet stopped spinning and dropped lifelessly to the ground, bouncing as it settled.

Sam squatted down and jumped straight up, traveling almost too fast for human perception. Bits of asphalt and dust followed him upward as he left the ground with ferocious intent. As quickly as he left the ground, he collided with the tail section of the first helicopter completely severing it from the rest of the aircraft.

As a burst of fire and smoke exploded from the severed section of the helicopter, it went into an uncontrollable spin. The piece of the tail that was knocked off came screaming down and crash landed on an adjacent roof to the turmoil below. The falling hunk of metal created a massive gash in the roof as the rotor blades cut through the layers of tar paper and insulation that covered the building.

 The rest of the helicopter drifted for a moment as Sam came smashing back to the ground, sending a ripple like shock wave outward and rupturing the pavement. The helicopter smashed into the side of a building eight stories above the street. A shower of glass came flying away from the building along with chunks of the body and propellers. Onlookers and cops scattered to avoid being sliced open by the falling debris. The helicopter lodged itself into the corner of the glass office building. The lights in the entire building flickered for a moment then suddenly went dark.

Completely unsatisfied by the blow dealt to the helicopter; Sam swiftly picked up an abandoned taxi cab by sinking his hands into the cheap metal that housed the front of it. With little difficulty at all, he chucked it towards the destroyed helicopter as easily as someone might throw an empty plastic trash can. After a brief and silent flight through the air, the car crashed into the helicopter causing a colossal explosion that sent more debris tumbling down onto the street and sidewalk that was now devoid of civillians.

The second helicopter backed away though still keeping the spotlight on the fuming shell of a man that Sam had become. Many of the police officers did not wait for an order to fire. They just witnessed this thing, this monster, take out a helicopter carrying several of their fellow officers. For them, that was all the permission they needed. The first wave came from behind him. It was a mix of shots from multiple guns. Some were police issued pistols; others were high caliber assault rifles. As they did so many times before, the bullets just bounced off him. But just as before, each time aggression was sent his way he sent it back with lethal consequences. In retaliation, he started throwing cars at them. As a baseball player scooping up one ground ball after another, he easily pitched cars parked at the meters on the roadside.

First a Mercedes, then a Tahoe and finally, a Hummer. All three vehicles flew through the air and struck their intended targets with pinpoint accuracy. The crushing sound of metal on metal as the cars smashed into the ground and the barricade of police cars was chilling and horrific all at the same time. Even more gut-wrenching was the sight of blood exploding from the wreckage of twisted metal and shattered glass. Every officer left started opening fire. Sam stumbled ever so slightly as the wave of bullets besieged him. Though none of them could break through his skin, the sheer amount of force from so many high powered weapons only posed a slight threat to his balance. He pushed back.

The deep purple glow once again consumed him and forced its way outward about ten feet from his body. Bullets couldn't penetrate through the dark and thick energy. Another thunderous roar belted from the bottom of his lungs toward the heavily armed aggressors. The rush of wind that followed picked up grime from the street and hurled it at them. Those without face masks were forced to cover their eyes from the blinding wall of wind and dirt that plowed at them.

Sam crouched at the knees and left the ground once more leaving behind crater of cracked concrete and asphalt. His trail of energy that remained in his wake looked like a cloud of mist falling from a rocket launched from deep under water. He had reached a height of around 100 feet before he began to fall. On his decent, the energy that surrounded him shifted to a bright green in a blast of light. It was apparent that his targets were the closest officers to him. There was no doubt about it; at this point that Sam was going to kill every one of them.

Without any warning, a bright white light shot across the sky from the north like a comet. It intercepted Sam in his decent. The light collided with him and took him out of sight in less than a second, leaving the police still cowering, wondering what just happened. Ever so reluctant to return to a fully upright position, the officers scanned the sky expecting the monster they were just battling to return with all of its rage and fury. The Chief gave the order to remain ready and not to let down their guard.

The soldier stood up first and surveyed the scene. He tried to assimilate what he was seeing and what he experienced a few moments ago. A very hollow look consumed his eyes. His face, covered with a mixture of dirt and the blood of his teammates that were slaughtered in the cavernous room below.

Scratches decorated the sides of his whisker covered cheeks. The fatigues that he was wearing were blood stained and beaten. Tiny holes were torn in them from all the chaos. Tired and devoid of any ability to process the situation with any real mental stability, he stood there as the other officers rose to their feet.

Everything began to move in slow motion as they started to scatter in an attempt to save their fallen brethren. Some were shouting, others simply fell to their knees crying. There were no real words in their minds to describe the carnage that decorated the street. Rarely had any of the officers seen an occasion to draw their guns from their holsters. The only real firefight action they had seen came from the firing range or simulated combat. This was a whole new level of extreme for them.

For the average civilian, this was far more violence than they would see in several lifetimes. Those that were not completely crippled by fear and awe took to the scene. Some to help, others broke out cell phones and cameras to document the breathtakingly horrendous event. Today would be a day for the history books. The day they saw a single man defy authority with such violent behavior and otherworldly power. This day would be the day they would call, "The First Day" in the years to come.

Meanwhile, the white burst of light that whisked Sam away deposited him onto some rooftop miles from the destruction and carnage he caused. Though he tried intently to free himself and attack this bizarre white light he couldn't move; he was paralyzed. Almost sedated. The anger left him. There was no more glow or screams of fury. Blind rage no longer filled his every breath. Sam peered deeply into the mesmeric light. He could barely make out the shape of a human looking figure.

He could not see its face or any distinguishable features for that matter. As the seconds passed, drowsiness washed over him like a wave kissing the shore. In his last moments of consciousness, the figure leaned in close and whispered

"All that power is pointless unless you can control it."

Chapter 9: The Soldier

Standing amid the carnage and wreckage that surrounded him on all sides, the soldier felt a hand on his shoulder. Warm and soothing, it posed no threat. He turned to see that the hand belonged to the police chief. He was a moderately tall black man. About six feet tall, 180 pounds, though the bulletproof vest made him look about 200 pounds. His hair was thick and peppered white. Bits and pieces of his close cut goatee were starting to turn white. From the gray in his hair to the wrinkled brow and crow's feet the soldier put the chief in his mid-fifties. His hand, placed on the soldier's shoulder, was callous and weathered. Not the hand of a man that lived in luxury, rather the hand of a man that spent too many winters laboring out in the cold. The veins were apparent and laced themselves in between the knuckles.
While pulling a cigarette from his lips and exhaling with a deep and raspy voice, the chief asked, "What's your name soldier?"

"Ruiz, sir," the soldier said "Sergeant Victor Ruiz."

"Well, Sergeant...why are you here?"

"I don't think I follow, sir."

"Let me rephrase that. Why is a soldier in full fatigues and body armor in the middle of the south side shopping

district? You are out of place," The chief took another drag from his half smoked camel.
He looked at Victor in an inquisitive manner.

"You got any idea what the hell that thing was?" the chief asked.

"He is a monster, sir," Victor responded.

"I don't believe in monsters, Sergeant?"

"I don't either sir, but I just watched one kill twenty-nine of my buddies down in that hole sir," said Victor with a look of anger and frustration scribbled across his face as he pointed to the massive hole in the middle of the street.

"You wouldn't happen to have another one of those would ya?" he asked gesturing towards the chief's cigarette.

"Of course."

The chief pulled the pack from his shirt pocket behind his bullet proof vest. He shook one to the top of the soft pack and offered it to Victor, then struck his lighter with the other hand. As he did so, he noticed a very visible shake in Victor's fingers. Clearly the sergeant had just gone through Hell. Even though it wasn't in the chief's personal nature to pry, it was part of the job and considering the circumstances, his job ruled out whatever he wanted.

"What's down in that hole sergeant?"

"I am afraid that information is classified." snapped a voice from behind the chief.

The chief turned to see a sharply dressed soldier walking towards him. He wasn't for sure, but the two stars on his shoulder told the chief that things were about to get very interesting. Victor snapped to attention, swiftly flicked his cigarette and fired off a crisp salute.

"General," said Victor

"At ease Sergeant. You won't be answering any more questions. The colonel over there will be debriefing you and taking your statement."

"Yes, sir" said Victor as he snapped back to attention and saluted again.

He nodded to the chief, and the chief did the same in return. With that, he headed toward the colonel leaving the general and the chief behind.

"Chief, I am gonna need you to clear your people out of here. This area is under the jurisdiction of the US government by order of the Pentagon," said the general.

The chief took a second to survey the scene. He saw the massive flood of military personnel that arrived. They filtered into the streets like ants pouring out of an ant hill that just got kicked.

Every single one of his men was having a similar conversation with someone in a military uniform. There was no way this was going to stay a police investigation or a standard crime scene and he knew it. With as much experience as he had, the chief was used to having the CIA or FBI stepping all over his toes. The events of this evening were far more severe than a murder or terror attack. Tonight he witnessed a massacre, and it was way above his pay grade.

"My officers and I are happy to cooperate. What can we do to help?"

"Chief, we appreciate the help. I will need all your men to clear the area. We could use your help keeping civilians and all the media out."

The General took the camouflaged hat off of his head and ran his hand through his very short GI-style hair. He took in a deep breath as his eyes fell toward the ground. As he exhaled, he looked up at the chief with a deep look of concern.

"Look," he said " This is just the beginning. I can't tell you much, but this city is getting ready for a complete shit storm. If our intelligence is on the money, this guy is going to do this again. I need any video of this as fast as you can get it to me. We've got to get this guy before he flips out again," stressed the General. "We are gonna be here for a while."

"Should I be worried about these people's safety?" he questioned.

"We have no real way of knowing what he is capable of or where he'll pop up next. We are just going to stop him before he has a chance to do this again," said the general. "Now if you'll excuse me..."

The general nodded to the chief and briskly walked past him. Walking away, he began barking orders to other military personnel.

Elsewhere, Victor sat down in a very barren room. There were only a couple of chairs and a table. This room was actually in a trailer that was pulled up by a diesel truck when the military showed up. It was a quiet room. He couldn't hear any sound from outside. He found it kind of strange that the United States army showed up within twenty minutes of the first shot fired in that underground room.

What made it even more strange is that the nearest military base is over 1 hour away. That means all these soldiers were out for coffee at the local Dunkin Donuts, or they knew this was going to happen. The situation was all definitely of the top secret variety. Hell, he needed to have top secret clearance just to get the job.

Victor heard the door crack open behind him. He knew the Colonel that walked into the room, so he saluted. He did not, however, recognize the egghead that walked in behind him. The Colonel was about five foot- ten inches tall with salt and pepper hair. His chest, covered in medals, and his face said that he earned every one of them. He was about 65 years old and had the wrinkles to prove it. The egghead was a completely different matter, though. Standing at about six foot three inches, this guy looked like he was fresh out of high school. He was clean shaved with thick black curly hair. Victor was able to tell that that he was of Indian descent, although he had no idea whether he was actually from India or somewhere else in the world.

The Colonel started the conversation, "Where is the rest of your team, Sergeant?"

Victor clenched his jaw in an attempt to hold back the overwhelming rush of emotion.

"They are all dead, sir," he said in a broken and shaky voice.

"I find that hard to believe Sergeant. Those were all highly trained men. Some of them even served under my command in Afghanistan."

"Yes, sir. We were all special operations Colonel. I did several tours with a couple of those men."

"So what killed them, Sergeant?"

"With all due respect sir, I was hoping you could tell me

what that thing was. It looked like some scrawny guy, but I've never seen anything that could do what that thing did. No way it was human."

"Why are you still alive Sergeant? If that thing did indeed kill all of your team, how come it didn't kill you?"

"Honestly Colonel, I have no idea. We did everything we could to kill it, though. First we put a bullet in its head. Then it got up and started picking us off like flies. Our rounds weren't even penetrating the target."

The egghead put the papers he held in his hand down on the table as he eagerly sat down in the chair across the table from Victor.

"You mean he was bullet proof!?" asked the young man.

"What kind of armor was he wearing?" the Colonel asked.

"He wasn't wearing any armor. Just a t-shirt and shorts. The rounds that made contact with him didn't seem to have any effect. He just stopped the other rounds before they could hit him. If I didn't see it with my own eyes, I wouldn't have believed it. The bullets just seemed to stop...right in front of him," said Victor.

The egghead got very wide eyed and leaned into him a little bit closer as he slid a picture in front of Victor. It was a picture of the flower that Sam and Frank were trying to steal

"Did he have this with him?" asked the egghead.

Victor looked up to the Colonel as if he were silently asking for permission to answer the question and at the same time asking who the hell this kid was. The Colonel cleared his throat and took a step toward the table.

"Sergeant, I would like for you to meet Hamned Gupta. He heads the scientific division of Project twelve, which is the research center you and the rest of your team were assigned to."

"That was a research center? It looked more like a bunker to me," Said Victor.

"That's because you never saw our lab, just the bunker," said Hamned in a very matter of fact tone.

The egghead was right. Victor didn't even know how he got assigned to that boring ass job. He was originally supposed to be on his third tour in Afghanistan kicking in doors. Two days before he shipped out his orders were changed, and he was assigned to that bunker.

Every day he would show up, swipe a security card that would open an elevator. Once inside the elevator, he would swipe his card again, and the elevator would take him to the bunker. Every day his job was to sit in that bunker with his other teammates in full gear and wait. It was the most boring assignment he had ever had.

For months, he sat in that bunker with those guys. They would play cards and talk about why the hell they thought they were there. He had never even seen what was on the other side of that black door until tonight. And now he wished he had never known.

"Yeah, he had that in his hand when we shot him the first time," Victor said, "But when he got back up he left it on the floor."

Hamned quickly looked up at the Colonel and jumped to his feet.

"That means it is still there; I need to get my team down there immediately, Colonel."

Once again the Colonel nodded and took a step back to clear the way for Hamned to exit. He quickly gathered his papers and the picture in front of Victor and walked out of the soundproof room.

As the door clicked shut behind him, Victor turned his attention back to the Colonel, who was taking a seat at the table.

"Sergeant, we've got to take this guy out before any more civilians get hurt. We assigned you to that post because of your outstanding record. I know you just lost a lot of buddies down in that hole. There will be time to mourn them later. Right now I need someone that has some experience with this thing to lead a strike team to eliminate this threat. Are you the man for that job?"

"Colonel, right now I would like nothing better," said Victor.

"Well, you are gonna get your chance. We will see to it you get time for some shut eye while we gather intel. You'll meet with your new team in the morning and then we will hit this bastard hard!" proclaimed the Colonel.

"Thank you, sir."

Both men rose to their feet, and Victor saluted the Colonel as he exited the room. Victor couldn't help but feel concerned. He was still quite shaken from the day's events. On top of that, he was exhausted. He hadn't slept. A mission to take down this monster seemed impossible. The strangest part of it all was that the violence he had witnessed was not what was weighing heaviest on his mind. It was the way that the monster was able to push thoughts into his head. He couldn't seem to get the vision of its burning white eyes out of his head.

Why did it leave him alive when it did not hesitate to kill everyone else? The truth of the matter was; he may never know. One thing was for certain, though, tomorrow he was going to have to face him again. He had never been so scared while thinking about a mission before.

What was he going to be able to do against something that could stop bullets in midair and run up walls? How do you stop something that can throw full-sized cars like toys? How do you kill the thing that chose not to kill you?

There was only one answer. Bigger guns and better strategy.

The next morning Victor woke up from a deep sleep in his hotel room. It was probably the best sleep he had ever gotten. Shockingly, the experience from the prior evening had not kept him awake at all. Almost as soon as his head hit the cheaply made pillow, he passed out. His dreams were that of his family. Amazing visions of romantic times with his wife and time spent playing with his children in the backyard of the house they always wanted but never had the financial means to buy.

There were no visions of violence. No feelings of fear, just calm, peaceful sleep. Victor woke twenty minutes before his alarm, which was highly unusual for him. He had trained his body through many years in the field to get every last drop of sleep he could because he never knew when he would get it again.

As was normal for his morning routine, he went straight into the shower. He found it to be the quickest way to wash away the grogginess away after a crappy night of sleep, but this morning it was simply to clean up. Before he even got in the shower, he turned on the TV and changed the channel to the local news. Listening to the local weathermen yammer on about how they thought the weather was going to be was somewhat of a morning pastime for him. Of course, they never got it right, and that was part of the entertainment of it. It also served as background noise to keep him out of his thoughts. It was a simple way to keep his mind clear of distractions and worries before missions.

Victor showered swiftly, then turned off the piping hot water. As he got out and wrapped a towel around his waist, he shoved a toothbrush in his mouth and exited the bathroom. He could hear the elevated and concerned voices of the newscasters talking about some horrific tragedy. He darted his eyes over to the TV only to get a harsh reminder of last night's events. There on the screen was a shaky cell phone video of the monster he had encountered only hours before. The media chose the perfectly horrifying clip of Sam throwing cars at the firing police officers.

The debate that was raging from one so called expert to another was if it was real or doctored footage. However, the consensus was that something horrible was going on, and the media were not allowed within ten blocks of the area. A massive chunk of downtown had been cut off from the public. Entire buildings were closed and evacuated. A no-fly zone had been established around the city to keep media helicopters away from the area. The military officially had no comment and the local police were citing problems with local gas lines hoping to ease the public.

In a brief press conference, the chief of police stated that the problem would be resolved quickly and that the closed part of the city would be reopened as soon as possible for business as usual.

Reporters on the street were stopping people and getting reactions from people. No one was buying it. Victor picked up the remote and started flipping through channels as he ran his toothbrush back and forth across his teeth. Every channel was the Same. One station after another was broadcasting with titles like "Mad Man On the Loose" and "A City in Chaos." Speculation was running wild.

Victor hit the power button on the remote and tossed it onto the bed. He walked over to the half steam covered mirror and continued to brush his teeth. He did hate the media. They always over sensationalized everything. It makes sense when you are in the business of telling stories, the scarier, the better. It will keep people tuned in. Still; he only had respect for war journalists. War journalists had the balls to show you the real shit. The type of stuff you saw in a movie theater when the shit hit the fan.

As he spit the mixture of toothpaste and saliva from his mouth into the sink, it started to hit him. Today he had to face that monster again. He rinsed his mouth and spat that into the sink as well. Looking up at the mirror, he could see the fear in his own eyes. It wasn't fear for himself; it was fear of how many of his men were going to die today. Every soldier signs on knowing that he is writing a blank check for nothing less than his life. Rarely are those checks cashed. Today, he was holding the check of every man on his team. Victor would be leading this mission, and if he screwed up, everybody on his team could die. This monster was nothing to be messed with.

A few minutes later Victor had finished putting on his fatigues and headed out the door of the cheap motel. The sun was sitting low in the early morning sky, but the temperature was already around 80 degrees. It was going to be a hot one, and the humidity was starting to bring sweat to his armpits. Today was about to suck. He bounced down the staircase and quickly hopped into the car that was waiting for him.

The car returned to the site of the previous evenings chaos and met with onlookers and press. Dozens of police were on site in the two blocks before the checkpoint to keep everything under control. As they moved closer to the site, the sea of blue police uniforms turned to a sea of light and dark brown digital camouflage. Each one heavily armed with assault rifles and body armor. Victor had seen several lockdown situations, and this is what they looked like. No one in and no one out without the proper credentials. The car was stopped three times before they made it all the way in and both the driver and Victor were asked to produce identification.

After ten minutes of driving and checkpoints, Victor was finally standing where he and Sam resurfaced onto the street the night before, although he wasn't able to see the hole anymore. It had several very tall makeshift walls erected around it. The debris was still there. The broken pieces of concrete and asphalt scattered across the ground. Among them were hundreds of bullets. People in civilian attire were taking photos and marking them. It seemed like a mundane task that could take all day because there were so many. One of the civilian workers put down a tag next to a cluster of bullets that said three hundred forty-two.

Victor raised his eyebrows in disbelief. He had seen this madness with his own eyes, but the truth was, his adrenaline and the urgency of all the evening's actions blurred the details.

There was a call from behind him, "Sergeant, we are ready for you."

A solid look of resolution came across his face. It was time to go to work. All his emotion and fear needed pushing away. There was no room for a scared little boy in the room full of men he was about to enter.

The room was indeed full of men, eighteen of them. Some he knew, others he didn't. But there was no doubt about it, this room was full of real men. Each one was Spec Ops. Each one had the look of war deep in his eyes. Every single man in there had seen action in the past two wars and some had prevented other wars from happening. No doubt about it, each one of them was a professional killer. They had all gotten to see the remains of the battlefield outside that room, and they had all watched the horrific footage of it taking place.

Victor stepped up to the front of the room and began to recount the events of the evening in detail to the room full of soldiers. Though none of them spoke, he could see the looks of concern on their faces as he told them about the soldiers that had died in the room below the city. Occasionally, one soldier would shoot a glance to the other in complete disbelief.

A glance that said, "This guy is full of shit." Victor saw it. He expected it. After all, what he was telling them sounded far-fetched. There was only one way to convince them of the truth. He stepped back for a moment and leaned over to whisper into the ear of the Colonel, who was standing beside him.

"They don't buy it. If we don't convince them of how strong this thing is, they are all going to die," He said.

"What do you suggest we do, Sergeant?"

"Show them the room, I assume everything is still there?"

"Cleanup is tomorrow; we are still documenting everything. You seriously want to show these men this before they head out?"

"They need to know," Victor whispered.

The Colonel paused, then looked Victor straight in the eyes for a moment. He was trying to process what Victor was saying to him. Showing a room full of dead soldiers to the next team didn't sound like too great of an idea to him. But Victor was right. These men needed to be prepared for combat against this thing. With a slight nod to Victor, the Colonel turned toward the men.

"On your feet gentlemen. We are going on a field trip," The Colonel barked.

Moments later all of the men stood in the dark cavernous room below the city. There was very little light. Most of it was generated from flashlights and portable LED lights on rickety stands. There was a faint bit of light coming into the room from the hole that Sam had created. The random pop of light from a camera flash disappeared into the deep recess of the room. From where they were standing, they could see the waterfall catching the faint glimmer of light as it forced its way across the large pool of water.

The streams of blood that led into that pool of water appeared as their eyes adjusted to the light. They could see the white sheets that covered the bodies of all the dead soldiers. Dead bodies were nothing new to them. These were highly desensitized soldiers. Victor turned to the men and addressed them.

"Last night I lost twenty-nine of my teammates down here. Twenty-nine highly trained soldiers dead in under a minute. Killed…by one guy. A single guy with no gun and no armor. We didn't have a single shot that penetrated. This is no joke gentlemen. We are up against a monster."

One of the soldiers stepped forward and asked, "One guy killed all these men with no gun?"

His tone still reeked of disbelief and sarcasm. It was still a lot for them to swallow. Victor walked over to one of the boulders where a soldier had landed in the mayhem. Atop the massive rock was a sheet with a bit of blood seeping through. He reached up and snatched the cover off the body to expose the dead soldier that had his throat ripped out. There was a general sense of discomfort that washed over the group. Several groans and moans slipped out from the pack of men.

"He didn't just kill them, gentlemen," Victor said "He ripped them apart with his bare hands. I know that is a tough pill to swallow, but I assure you it's very true. Later today we are going to be tracking this guy down. We are under very strict orders to kill on sight."

"Sir. I see shell casings all over the floor. Looks like you guys squeezed off a lot of rounds. How many times did you hit the target?" asked one of the soldiers.

"Not once." Said Victor with a bit of disbelief still in his voice. "We threw close to a thousand rounds at him. We even launched grenades at him, and they had no effect."

The men grumbled for a brief moment. Victor expected

no less. He had just told them that this guy they were going after was bullet proof. The whole idea would be completely unbelievable to him too if he hadn't experienced it himself.

"This guy is faster than anything you have ever encountered. He was able to move so fast that our eyes couldn't keep up with him. He is wicked strong and mean as all Hell. Make no mistake gentlemen, if you give him the chance he will rip you apart too."

Chapter 10: Reality Check

"When I was a child, I talked like a child; I thought like a child, I reasoned like a child. When I became a man, I put childish ways behind me." - 1 Corinthians 13:11 -

Michael let go of Sam's hand as he returned from his very powerful flashback. The weight of what Sam experienced was immediately apparent on his face. The tears began to flow almost instantly as he scrambled backward from Michael.

"That was a hell of a ride. Right?" Michael said with a shit-eating grin strapped across his face.

He seemed quite pleased with himself having just shown Sam a nightmarish recap of the previous evening's events. Recording the events of the world the job he was built for. To record and report. Sam settled to his butt with legs out in front and breathing heavily.

"I saw all those people dying...and he was just ripping them apart...so much blood," sobbed Sam.

"Uhhhh...'He'...was just ripping them apart?" questioned Michael.

"He just made me watch. That bastard wouldn't let me close my eyes," said Sam

"Yeah....um...you are talking about that murderous rampage that happened downtown with all the soldiers and police? Right?"

Michael raised an eyebrow in a manner suggesting that his curiosity had peaked. Naturally, he expected a bit of disconnection from the event, but this was interesting.

"Hate to be the bearer of bad news pal, but that was you that was acting like a ravenous fool on a rampage."

"What?" Sam said in a lost and rather dazed fashion.

The single word that just escaped his lips laced with such confusion and disbelief that it almost reeked of honesty. Cocking his head a bit to the side Michael started questioning how Sam was processing this situation. After all, it was a lot to take in. He had just woken up with no memory of the previous evening, covered in blood, senses in overdrive.

On top of all that, a man claiming to be an angel threw him half a city block and showed him a scene that looked like something from a sci-fi, horror film that started with him getting shot in the head. Michael could understand how it was a bit much to take in so early in the day. Nevertheless, he knew today was going to be one for the history books and he needed Sam to be somewhat grounded in reality.

"What exactly did you see Sam?" he questioned.

Sam sat motionless with a thousand-yard stare in his eyes. Michael squatted down to his level and peered into those hollow eyes. He reached out and lightly smacked Sam across the cheek.

"Hey...space cadet!"

Sam lost the gaze and looked up at Michael.

"What did you see?" he questioned again.

Sam stood up and pushed past Michael as though he were walking away. Refusing to speak to Michael was a skill that he had developed through many years of ignoring strangers in the city and people he just didn't like. He wanted to tell him what he saw. He also was desperate for answers, but the last thing he wanted was to talk to a complete stranger claiming to be otherworldly.

"Sam, wait..." Said Michael.

Sam made it only a few steps before he came to a complete stop. Pausing for a moment, he began to process the events of the morning. He gazed down at his shirt that was splattered with blood that he knew was his, then down to his hands which were still wrapped in the blood-soaked fabric from his bathroom. As he removed the cloth, he was astonished to see that the wounds on the palms of his hands completely healed. Not even a mark was there. All that remained was the dried and coagulated blood that filled the grooves and creases of his palm prints. Slowly pulling his fingers inward into fists he could see the blood trapped under his fingernails. Zooming into it with his newfound sight, he could see that it didn't match his own.

Taking in a deep breath, Sam could smell the stench of death on him, though it was ever so faint it was undeniable. Sewer water and the smell of shit filled his nose as he focused on the odors that were tickling his senses. He knew something was up, but he wasn't the guy that killed all those people. He knew it with every fiber of his being.

The fact that this stranger was telling him all this bullshit struck a chord deep inside of him. He was appalled and insulted by the crap this guy was trying to shove down his throat. A swell of anger started swirling deep inside his belly. It was anger that was much more powerful than he was used to. That anger took him over faster than he realized. Clenching his jaws lock tight, he spun around and rushed Michael again. This time snatching him up by the collar with one hand and dangling him from the edge of the roof.

"What the FUCK did you do to me?" he barked.

"I didn't do anything to you," said Michael.

Looking down at the concrete, several stories below, he reached up and scratched his face in a very nonchalant manner. "But if you are going to drop me…"

Without a second of hesitation, Sam let go of Michael's collar and left his fate to gravity. There was no flailing from the falling angel. He simply looked down and accepted what was happening. Shoving his head backward and arching his back, Michael performed a laid out backflip that would have left Olympic level divers envious. Finishing the flip and landing gently on the concrete in a very heroic fashion, the only sound that could be heard was the rustling of his clothes.

Looking up at Sam and standing there on the edge was a frustrating sight. The fall was nothing for him. Michael was sure Sam thought he would go splat. Not only that, but he didn't give it a second thought. He just dropped him mid-sentence. Sam was certainly not following the same path of those before him. These sudden bursts of aggression were not supposed to be happening. In fact, he should have been getting calmer by the second. At least, that is what happened to Rah and Ismael, he thought. Something funny was going on. One thing was for sure after the thousands of years he had spent on this earth; humans never ceased to amaze him.

Michael leaped from the ground with the same grace and elegance that he had landed. Effortlessly, he flew up to the rooftop and landed just behind Sam. Just as his feet made contact with the ground, Sam spun again quickly. This time, he took a swing at Michael. With all of his might, Sam rocketed a punch directly at Michael's nose. It was a fruitless effort. The angel simply raised his hand and caught the punch. There was a thunderous connection between the palm of his hand and Sam's fist.

It created a loud clap and a slight burst of air. Sam's eyes, billowing with anger, gazed at Michael from beneath his brow. With an expressionless look in his eyes, Michael squeezed down on the fist that was in his hand. There was a slight cracking sound. He could tell that he had already broken a few bones in Sam's hand, yet there was no sign of pain on his face. Whatever was causing him to be so aggressive had a strong hold on him.

As much as he wanted their first encounter to be a pleasant and easy one, it seemed it was going to be just the opposite. Sam was definitely in a state of denial and wasn't willing to have any discussion at all. Given his heightened state, reasoning with him was out of the question. The unfortunate part of it all was that Michael had so many incredibly important things to tell him. Like where his power was coming from and what to expect. But all that would have to wait for the moment. Sam needed a reality check, and fast. He was very strong in his new state of being. Perhaps stronger than he knew, but Michael was an angel, and at the moment his abilities were far superior to Sam's.

An all-out brawl was out of the question as he could not risk aggravating the monster that he saw last night. He needed to let the air out of Sam's tires without any more collateral damage. Michael had the perfect solution. It was time for an elevation change.

Gripping him by the wrist, Michael rocketed into the air with Sam in tow. He wasn't about to fight with this human. He couldn't reason with him. So he decided to suffocate him. Just a bit. It truly seemed like the only option. The pair plowed through the clouds above at blistering speeds. Onward and upward Sam looked down as the world below him became increasingly smaller with every second. His natural instinct was to fight, but logic told him that a fall from this high was certain death. The air was freezing and grew colder with every moment that past. All of this was so surreal. Only a few minutes ago he was waking up, and now he is being rocketed into the sky by a very well dressed stranger.

His anger began to give way to fear. The pain in his hand started to set in alongside a rather ferocious case of the shivers. He could feel the ironclad grip of Michael's hand wrapped around his wrist. When would this guy stop he thought. He tried to shout at Michael to stop, but the roar of the air rushing by them as they climbed higher and higher was drowning out all the sound coming from his frozen mouth.

He was so cold that he could barely pronounce any words as his tongue lay in his mouth like an icy slab of meat behind his already numb lips. And then it hit. He saw a slight sparkle in his vision, and then another. There was a wave of bliss that came over him as those sparkles multiplied and filled his vision. Without him even noticing, he slipped into unconsciousness.

Sam came to in a very peaceful manner. He could feel the wind on his face and the air was nice and clean. He was a bit cold, but the summer sun was shining directly on him, and its rays felt warm and soothing after his very cold adventure. He began to open his eyes and noticed that he wasn't standing on the ground. With his arms dangling above his head and the blood that was putting pressure on his face, he felt as though he was hanging in the air still. That iron-clad grip that was previously around his wrist was now around his ankle.

He was indeed still in the air, only now he was upside down with an up close and personal view of a very expensive pair of shoes. His eyes darted around in a frenzied attempt to get a grip on his whereabouts. Not much had changed from before his slip into the dark abyss of unconsciousness. He was still incredibly far from the ground though now it appeared only to be a thousand feet or so; but at that height, who can tell. As he looked up, or down as his orientation would have it, he saw Michael's face smiling back at him.

"Let's make a deal. You stop acting like a raging freak, and I won't drop you. Sound like a plan?"

It didn't take much thought. Sam couldn't fly, and he didn't feel like dying. Michael's offer seemed pretty solid to him. Sam looked down at the ground once more and then shot his attention back up to Michael's face.

"I'm cool with that. But can you, at least, turn me around? This is kind of a scary way to have a conversation, "said Sam.

Michael reached down and grabbed Sam by the arm. With minimal effort, he spun him around till they were face to face.

"You can fly," Sam said, "This is so trippy."

"What did you expect? I am an Angel."

"Yeah, but you don't have any wings," Sam was quick to point out.

"I do. You just can't see them yet." Michael responded.

"Yet?" Sam questioned.

"You have to give your abilities time to mature. Before you went all aggro, I was about to tell you what was happening to you. Instead, you decided to throw me off a building."

"About that...."

"No apologies needed. You are not the first person that has tried to kill me. Listen… would you mind if we had this conversation on something a bit closer to the ground?" asked Michael.

"I would prefer it." Said Sam

The ground has never felt so good, thought Sam as they touched down. Where they were standing wasn't exactly the ground, though. Michael had set them down on top of the tallest building in the city. This building stood only blocks from Sam's rampage the night before, and he could clearly see the aftermath of the carnage from the previous night. They were standing on top of the Cain building. A marvel of modern architecture. It was pretty basic on the outside, but the inside was a technophile's dream.

The city was elated when The Cain Corporation decided to set up its global headquarters in the heart of their meager little downtown area. The mayor practically held a parade. Since then, the city had prospered financially, and many of the businesses in the downtown area owed their very existence to The Cain Corporation, including the restaurant that Sam worked at...until last night.

Even in the middle of summer, the air was still brisk at twenty-three stories above the city. The cool breeze that shot across the rooftop did wonders for Sam's state of mind. He had always been a fan of the wind and the fresh air. It helped keep him calm and relaxed his mind. He did not know why. It just did. Strategically speaking, Michael figured this would still give him a tactical advantage if Sam lost his cool again. A fall from this height would certainly kill him. Plus, there was nothing of any real value to damage up here and no press or random people to whip out a cell phone and start shooting video. No, this was a safe place for this all important discussion to take place.

"Sam, we have a lot to talk about. I really need you to listen. I can help you make sense of what's going on with you and why you saw whatever it was that you saw in the vision I gave you. But... if you don't stay calm, I am going to throw you off of this building. Plain and simple."

Sam's eyes snapped over to Michael in a very "say what?" fashion. He turned and walked over to the edge and cautiously leaned out to get a good sense of how far it was down to the ground. The feeling of fear began to swell in him. It took root in his lower abdomen and shot a falling sensation up his spine then forced him to clench his jaw.

"You would throw me off this roof?" he asked.

"Yes, if it will save me time," he answered.

"You keep saying you don't have a lot of time, are you gonna be late for something?"

"Nope, I am never late for anything. I am very much an Alpha kind of person."

"But you are an angel, not a person, right?" questioned Sam

"I am not here to discuss me. We are here to talk about you. Now come away from the edge and let's talk."

Michael motioned Sam to come closer to him. Taking one last peek over the edge, he craned his neck out as far as it would go and peered down the edge of the building. Just then, a blast of wind blew across the top of the building and caused Sam to lose his balance ever so slightly. He stumbled a bit and quickly scurried backward to safer ground. Eyes wide open, he took in a very deep breath and sighed relief on the exhale. Turning towards Michael, he got a very focused look in his eyes. He had no intention of getting thrown from this roof. Even more important than the threat of an angel hurling him from the top of a twenty-three story building was the more pressing question; why on earth was an angel stalking him and what did it have to do with these dramatic changes that happened to him?

"What is happening to me?" Sam questioned.

"You are evolving."

"Evolving into what? Tell me I am not turning into a lizard."

"Hardly." Said Michael "You are turning into a god."

"Bullshit," said Sam "God isn't real. I don't believe in God. No such thing."

"Well, you are right and wrong all at the same time. God, as all these silly religions have him made out to be, is a load of crap. But the real GOD," said Michael as he made the quotation signs with his fingers "does exist. He is VERY real."

"I think you're full of it." Said Sam. "Prove it."

"Really? You were just hoisted in the sky by an angel. You are only alive because of a flower, you killed a crap load of people that were shooting thousands of rounds of ammunition at you, and lived to see another day. I would say the concept of God is open for discussion at this point...wouldn't you?"

"A flower? What flower?" asked Sam.

"You don't remember the flower from last night do you?"

"Pppppfftt. I told you, all I remember is being forced to watch that thing kill all those people. It was such a crazy nightmare. To be honest, I feel like I'm still dreaming."

"I think we are going about this the wrong way. Why don't we start with you telling me about this dream you had last night?" Michael questioned.

"Sure. Ever since I was a kid, I have had dreams like this. They are all slightly different, but the same. They stopped right when I became a teenager, but last night was the first one I have had in a while. It was way more intense than I have ever had.
 It was crazy, Frank and I were in this cave like place. Lots of water. Then we used some dynamite to blow open this door. It was more like a big rock, though. Next thing I know there were all these soldiers and they shot Frank. That part felt real. Almost like it actually happened, you know? Then all of a sudden I'm in the

pit. It is like this place I would always start the dreams in. It's full of this thick black sludgy crap and its super hard to get out of, and it sticks to you like glue. Once I get out of the pit, there is this thing there."

"Most times he tries to speak to me, but I can't understand anything he is saying. When he talks, it's like my gut hurts and I feel sad and angry. This time, it was a bit different, though. When I got out of the pit, I was in the same place, but it was all on fire and burnt. Even the water was on fire. All I could smell was sulfur and ash."

Sam continued, "Then I noticed that I was standing on the ceiling looking down at everything. All the soldiers were there, and Frank was dead on the ground. But that thing was standing where I was standing. He looked up at me and laughed. These black slimy ropes flew out of the pit and grabbed me so tight I couldn't move," Sam's mental attitude became excited.

"Then that thing started killing everybody. Very scary and very real! Every time I would try to close my eyes and not watch, but more of those oily black ropes would come and hold them open. It truly felt like this was happening. Then, we were in the middle of the city, and he was throwing cars at people." Sam explained.

"You mean… like right over there?" Michael pointed to the destroyed area that was sectioned off a couple of blocks away.

"Sort of. But it didn't look like that. Once that thing showed up, everything caught on fire or was burnt and crumbling. Everything was destroyed; it was like being inside a furnace or in Hell or something like that. It just all seemed so real. I wanted him to stop killing all those people but.... I couldn't do anything to stop him. It was a pretty fucked up dream." Sam paused for a moment.

"So tell me more about this God thing." he petitioned Michael.

"Sam, what you saw was you going berserk."

"Riiiiiiiiiiight…" Sam said in a sarcastic fashion.

"Your friend Frank is dead, and you killed all those people."

"You know, for a brief second, I thought we were gonna talk about what was going on with me. Now I see this is still a dream. There is no way this is real. You're an angel, with no wings I might add. You swear that I killed all those people from the first part of my dream. You are telling me that I am evolving into a God and that my best friend is dead. What about this doesn't seem like a dream to you?"

"Good point." agreed Michael.

He could see that Sam was rationalizing this experience. And he was doing quite a good job at it. From the average man's viewpoint, none of the things Sam had gone through in the past 24 hours would fall into the category of real. And because he didn't have a first-hand account of what happened last night, it gave him an even greater ability to distance himself from everything and made it easier to come to the natural conclusion that this was all a dream. But unfortunately, nothing could be further from the truth. Every bit of this was real. Michael just needed to convince him of it.

"You seem to be pretty up to speed on what dreams are and how they work, right?" Michael questioned.

"Ten years of court-ordered therapy made me somewhat of a dream enthusiast," Sam replied.

"How do dreams work then?"

"Basically, the subconscious mind regurgitates information you have gathered and arranges it into a sequence of images. Some people think it's the brain's way of passing important info back to the conscience. Others say it is just garbage," Sam sputtered this info out to Michael as he had to so many others.

It made for a great conversational piece and would often get his foot in the door with any ladies that happened to be a part of the conversation. While he did know quite a bit about dreams, he managed to filter most of it into a cleverly arranged series of questions and answers that were custom designed to get him into an unsuspecting pair of panties.

"So what do you think? Is this dream a message or a bunch of garbage?" Michael asked.

"I haven't decided yet. When I figure it out, I'll let you know."

Maybe convincing Sam he wasn't dreaming was not the smartest way to handle the problem, Michael thought to himself. If he believes he is dreaming, he is much more likely to accept the information that is being given to him. Couldn't hurt to try. At least for now.

"Well, if this is a dream, it's about to get a lot crazier. Let me bring you up to speed on the past few days," Michael paused for a brief moment.

His eyes darted upward and started shifting left and right as he raised his brow. There was some slight gesturing and mumbling as though he were trying to explain something to himself.
"Don't tell me you went to all this trouble and had no idea what to say," Sam took a sarcastic stab at the angel.

"No. No. I know what to say. I am just one petal behind, and I am trying to take out all the pageantry and what not."

"One petal behind?" the young man questioned.

"Right. I guess that's as good a place as any to start." Michael cleared his throat. "Last night you and your friend stole a flower from a place that only a few people even knew existed. While you think it was only a dream, it was quite real."

"Nope. That was just a dream. I have had dreams like that before," protested Sam.

"Then how do you explain all that blood on your shirt?"

"Nosebleed. I get them all the time."

"What about all the blood on the back of your shirt?"

Sam began to crank his head around to look at his back. He even pulled his shirt over his shoulder towards the front to get a better view. Michael was right. There was more blood on the back of his shirt than on the front.

He spun his head back around to look at Michael with a confused and inquisitive look that said, "You've got my attention."

"But come to think of it, you didn't steal the flower because it was yours to start with. Kind of a destiny thing you could say. Ismael wanted you to have it..."

"Who's Ismael?" asked Sam

"We'll get to that in a few minutes. Back to the flower. The flower bonded with you right about the same time that bullet pushed your brains out onto the floor."

"Wait, what do you mean? You mean I got shot? In the head? Riiiiiiight!!!!" Sam stated quite sarcastically.

"Well, you don't have to believe it to make it real. However, the truth of the matter is, you were shot in the head. Your blood-bonded with the flower." Michael confidently stated.

Looking back down at his crusty blood-soaked shirt, Sam pinched it and pulled it away from his chest just a bit. It was slightly crunchy and didn't snap back the way a fresh, clean one would. He let out a small sound of wonderment.

"Hmph. So If I got shot, why am I still here having this conversation? And why don't I remember it?"

"The flower resurrected you. It is called an ascension. As for why you don't remember, not for sure on that one," Michael scratched the stubble on his face.

"The flower is like a free life in one of your video games. Every time you die, it will bring you back to life. When it does, you come back twice what you could have been before."

"You mean what I was?" interjected Sam

"No. I quite literally mean what you could have been. Each one of you clever little monkeys is uniquely different. Even when there are over seven billion of you on this rock, you are all slightly set apart from one another. However, you all have similar traits in common. You can only run so fast, lift so much, smell things that are a certain distance away," explained Michael.

"So you mean physical limitations?" Sam chimed in.

"It's more than that. You are only capable of becoming so smart, or having a finite understanding of any given situation. Your mental and even your emotional state is limited by the human condition. However, when the flower brings you back, it allows you to max out that human state of being, and then double it."

"So you are saying I am twice as fast and twice as smart as I was yesterday?"

"No. I am saying you are twice as fast as the fastest human being ever to walk this planet. You are twice as smart as the smartest human that has ever lived," emphasized Michael.

"Uhhhhhhh....I don't feel smarter, or faster...I still feel the same...."

Sam suddenly began to experience an "AH-HA" moment. He thought about what happened a few moments ago when he slammed Michael into the wall, and earlier when he destroyed the bathroom sink. He looked down at his hands. They had completely healed after having been ripped open only a few minutes ago by the shattered porcelain. Michael's words carried an immense amount of logic suddenly. Michael could see it dawning on Sam's face. The truth was hitting him like a ton of bricks.

"Freaky, isn't it?" said Michael. "Currently, it's all new to you, so it won't work unless you make it work. At first, you won't just walk around having epiphanies with your coffee in the morning. It will take a bit of time before you can use all your power without thinking about it. But a few things will come naturally like they did earlier when you tried to knock my head off."

"Sorry about that. You caught me off guard," apologized Sam.

"You should have seen what Ismael did the first time he got angry. It was pretty impressive for a monkey."

"So basically, what you're saying is I just became fucking AWESOME!!!!"

"Yes...sort of. But there is a lot more to it than that..." Michael stated.

"How many languages can I speak?" Sam interrupted again.

"I don't know. How many could you speak yesterday?"

"One."

"Then that's how many you can speak today," answered

Michael.

A puzzled look streaked across the face of the new genius, "Wait, what? I thought I was all super smart now. I don't get it."

"It doesn't work like that Sam. Your brain is not the freaking library of congress all of the sudden. There is a difference between learned knowledge and reasoned knowledge. There is also common sense or experienced knowledge. A human brain is a problem-solving tool. When it comes to figuring things out, you will excel without any effort. However, things like statistics, pointless facts, languages and anything else that involves learning or memorizing, you have to learn it. Your intelligence is not measured by what you currently know, but by what you are capable of figuring out." Michael explained.

"All that having been said, you could learn ten languages today if you had a chance to study them. Physical actions will come easily to you at this stage in your ascension. Your body can do amazing things because it already did them before, just not at the level you are currently at. As time goes on, you will begin to notice dramatic changes in your mind and body. It just takes time."

"Well, that's cool and kinda crappy at the same time. I am super smart and don't know a damn thing. Go fucking figure," Sam complained.

"Not true. There are things you are highly knowledgeable at right now. Math will be very easy for you. You will not need to study or learn this. It will come naturally. Math is the common language of the universe. It's hardwired into your brain from birth. One plus one equals two no matter where you are."

"Great!!! Now I can go back to school and get that degree I have wanted for so long." Said Sam.

Michael could cut Sam's sarcasm with a chainsaw. It was very apparent that he was not at all impressed with the new strengths that he had acquired. All the better Michael thought. Anything to keep him from losing it like he did the night before. Michael was not joking when he said that Ismael's first angry spat was impressive, but it paled in comparison to the rampage that Sam went on. He was only on the first petal, and he had no clue what would happen next time. Michael was faced with a very serious issue. He needed to figure things out before Sam could spread his wings again. It was clear that this young man had some serious hidden anger issues buried deep inside.

Ismael didn't mention anything like this to him beforehand. However, he knew that everything Ismael did had a spider web of reasons behind it. He just hoped he could get it all figured out before Sam encountered any repercussions from last night. Michael knew that if he freaked out again, it would end poorly.

Now was not the right time to fill Sam in on absolutely

everything there was to know. He was a bit too snarky at the moment and needed some time to get a grip on some of his new abilities. Besides, it was not his job to protect Sam from anyone or vice versa. He was simply there to record and guide. The only reason he was telling Sam what he had was because Ismael told him to. He would rather be at the bar. In fact, there was a bottle of bourbon calling his name right now.

Michael could only handle so much of someone being more sarcastic than him, "Sam... Let's stop for the day. I need a drink."

"An angel that drinks. Now I know I am dreaming. Fine. I am going to enjoy the rest of this dream. How do we get down?"

"Take the stairs," Michael said as he began to float away.

"Take the stairs he says.... This dream is fucking stupid."

Chapter 11: Accepting Fate

Standing there, hundreds of feet in the air, atop the roof of one of the largest buildings in the city surrounded by the massive amounts of air conditioners and things that hummed with the sound of productivity, Sam began to ponder his current situation. This dream had taken an interesting turn, he thought. How do I get down from here? He hadn't even gotten to brush his teeth, and he was quite anxious to get out of these blood-soaked clothes. First thing first. How to get down?

Since this was a dream, he could simply jump from the roof. However, he was kind of enjoying this dream and was afraid the fall would stir him from his slumber. Then he thought that every roof has a door that leads to floors below. A quick pan and scan of his surroundings revealed such a door. A few steps later and Sam placed his hand on the handle only to discover the obvious. It was locked. Sam thought this was the silliest thing ever.

"Why would you lock a door that goes nowhere?" He thought to himself. Even if someone were to find their way up here, what would they steal?

The moment he finished his thought his head filled with a ridiculous amount of answers. Suicide, base jumping, sabotage, snipers, activists, graffiti artists, the list went on and on. Now he understood why the door was locked, but it did not help his situation. He placed his hand back on the handle and gave it a quick jiggle, only to have the knob come off in his hand. He had peeled it from the door like it was made of tissue paper. Looking down at the handle in his hand, thoughts began to flood his head. The first was amazement. He was still completely unused to his new found strength and the fact that he could do this so easily was rather amusing.

The second set of thoughts shot through his mind faster than the first. These were thoughts of irritation. He had just ripped the handle off the door. How the fuck was he supposed to open the door now? Sam shook his head side to side ever so slightly. With a massive burst of power, he spun 180 degrees and threw the handle as hard as he could. It rocketed away like a missile out of sight. His tantrum didn't stop there. He screamed at the top of his lungs, "MOTHER FUCKER!!!!!!!!"

Sam once again spun 180 degrees and kicked the door in anger and frustration. While he was expecting the door to make a loud sound and sting his foot, it did something much more dramatic. With barely an effort at all, he had kicked the door so hard that it became concave as it rocketed from its hinges and bounced down the 20 stairs behind it. It did indeed make a loud sound. Far louder than he had expected and it made a lot more of it. Sam placed his hands on top of his head, eyes wide and posture crouched. Two words slipped across his lips. "Holy shit."

He knew he was going to get busted. So much sound was bound to set off an alarm. But as far as Sam was concerned, this was a dream. And a rather lucid one at that. The chances of there being an alarm were slim to none. At least, that's what he had convinced himself of...just before the alarm began to scream. With ear-piercing volume, a building-wide alarm cracked through the wind-whipped air. Swiftly, Sam's hands covered his ears in pain as he dropped to his knees. The sound shredding his ear drums was utter Hell. He couldn't hear anything beyond the soul crushing shrill of that goddamned alarm.

He knew he had to get off this rooftop, and he wasn't about to go over the edge. The only way out was down those stairs. Staggering to his feet, hands still covering his ears as if it made a difference, he darted toward the door and down the stairs. His feet rapidly negotiated the steps one after another. The concrete muffled the sound from the outside but the ear-shattering racket continued to echo down the stairs as if it were chasing him one flight at a time.

If this were a perfect dream, he would be able to make it to street level without being noticed. However, nothing in this dream had gone as planned or as it should have and he expected trouble at any moment.
His expectations were met by an ever so faint sound that was made several floors below him. His newly found gifted hearing picked up on it the instant it was made. This sound was the sound of a door slamming open against the wall. There were several very large men rushing out of it and storming the steps aggressively. From the sound of it, they were coming up.

The rattle of keys and the friction of body armor on top of fabric quickly overtook the sound of the hideous alarm that had been pounding in his head. Somehow, he had managed to dial his hearing into all of the minuscule sounds that were echoing off the dull, thick concrete walls. The sound of material rubbing together, the jostling of full ammunition clips moving around in pouches. Sam's ears could pick up the sound of air being pushed out of lungs as it flew past the mouth and from behind protective masks.

"This is amazing," he thought to himself. He only wished more dreams were like this. The clarity and detail in this dream were far superior to any other dream he had ever had. So much so that he thought about what a shame it would be to wake up from something like this, only to go back to the supermundane life he was living in what he believed to be the real world. It seemed to be a no-brainer that he should push the boundaries of this dream world and find out just what he was capable of.

To accomplish that, he was going to need a serious challenge. Why not charge at the several men that were making their way to him via the stairwell. That seemed like an adequate challenge. Besides, what was the worst that could happen? If, for some strange reason he was hurt badly or died, he would just wake up. His mind was made up. If he had in fact performed the dastardly feats Michael had told him of earlier, this should be a cakewalk.

Moments later, Sam rounded the corner in the stairwell and there stood his challenge. Five men in tactical gear. He had made a ton of noise coming down the last couple of flights in hopes that they were prepared for him when he got there. He certainly got his wish. The only thing that caught Sam off guard was the fact that they were so heavily armed. He honestly could not think of a single time in his short-lived life that he had seen a security guard in body armor carrying an M4 carbine assault rifle. It was a bit out of place, but then again so was he.

"Don't move...!" shouted one of the armored guards. "...Stay where you are and lay down on your stomach with your hands on your head!" He barked.

Sam smirked a little bit. He could see fifty ways in his head to get past these guys. Twenty-two of those ways sent them all to the hospital; the rest involved killing, at least, one of them. The guard shouted his commands again, only, this time, his intent was a bit more forceful.

"Get down on the ground with your hands behind your head...or I will shoot you!"

Sam's smirk widened into a full-blown smile.

"You have until the count of three."

Sam's adrenaline was racing. He could hear the anxiety in the guard's voice. He knew this guard was going to shoot him if he didn't follow the orders being shouted at him. The guard was afraid as well, though. It was pouring out of his sweat glands and from behind his eyes.

"One..."

Still not budging an inch, Sam tuned his ears into the heartbeats of all the guards. However, the one shouting at him had a heart that was racing; it paled in comparison to what appeared to be some of the most inexperienced guards in the group. To Sam, it sounded like a symphony of muted drums that were all out of sync.

"Two..."

Should he wait until three? He felt a powerful urge surging through his body. If he jumped the gun and attacked, they all might start firing. He felt very confident that he could move fast enough to dodge a single bullet, but dodging multiple bullets might be a bit tough.

"Three!"

Without a single second of pause, the guard pulled the trigger. His M4 discharged a single bullet. Sam could see it coming out of the barrel in slow motion, being propelled forward from the gun by a blast of hot air and fire. It was a very surreal experience. He had seen this kind of slow motion on tons of shows on the Discovery Channel, as well as, the internet, but now he was getting to see it firsthand with his own eyes. The bullet was traveling so slow that he could see the rotations and the air distortion around it as the ultra-hot piece of metal rocketed at him at a snail's pace.

How exactly to handle this situation? Which one of the dozens of scenarios should he choose from? Should he side-step the bullet, then leap down the stairs with a flurry of punches and Kung Fu style kicks? Or maybe he should race down the stairs and steal all their guns before they can even figure out what happened? There were so many options before him, and it was hard to decide. He may never get an opportunity like this again. He certainly did not want to regret it later by thinking of some incredibly witty thing he should have said or done. Alas, Sam decided the best option was to wing it. Just freestyle through this event and let the chips fall where they may.

He did not intend to hurt them. Even though they fired a bullet at him, he felt it was a far more noble to just rough them up a bit and see to it that they still got to it go home for dinner tonight with their families. No sense in killing anybody. It is not as if the bullet was going to hit him or anything; he thought to himself.

As the bullet crawled ever closer to him, Sam figured it was about time to spring into action. He felt like a character on the big screen, like a newfound hero discovering his powers for the first time. However, something was bizarre. Though his perception of time was accelerated, his body's ability to keep up with that perception of time was nonexistent. He was not able to move. He was sending all the signals from his brain to his body. Though they were moving at twice the speed of what they normally should, they couldn't beat the two-thousand-nine-hundred-seventy feet per second that the bullet was traveling

He might as well have been paralyzed. All he could do was stand and watch as the bullet crept ever closer to him. It was traveling towards his left thigh. The guard had not intended to kill him, but rather wing him instead. Sam was once again in Hell. This bullet was going to rip right through the center of his thigh. He knew it was going to hurt. Nevertheless, that wasn't what made it so bad. His brain was making a ridiculous amount of calculations. Throughout the dreadfully long time it took the bullet to travel this far, Sam's mind had told him that once the bullet made contact with his leg, the signal would reach his brain almost instantly. He knew that the speed at which a touch signal travels to the brain was about three hundred fifty feet per second. He somehow managed to remember that from his biology class in the tenth grade. A class he had slept through. But he wondered if this was going to happen faster due to his doubled state of being.

His brain was telling him the size of the impact wound, the amount of blood he was going to lose, how long it was going to take him to bleed to death from a wound like this and so on and so forth. Just then he remembered something; this was just a dream. The worst that would happen was that he was simply going to wake up and think about how wild all this was in the first place.

Then it hit him. The bullet that is. Square in the thigh, just as he thought it would. He wasn't able to dodge it at the very last second. And he was right about a few things. The bullet made the same size hole he thought it would. He lost exactly as much blood as he predicted down to the drop. His theory that the pain would travel faster was accurate. It did indeed travel twice as fast as he thought it would.

But at that moment, when that bullet pierced his skin and began to destroy any and all flesh that was in its path, Sam came to a startling revelation.

This was not a dream.

He knew this because, in dreams, you can't create new information. Your mind will simply regurgitate what it already has seen and experienced. Before this very moment, he could have rationalized anything he had seen and felt; the building, the fantastical experience with Michael, the stairwell, the gunshot and everything else. But this pain, it was unlike anything he had ever felt before. Broken bones, stitches, knocked out teeth, cuts, scrapes, bangs, and bruises. Nothing he had ever felt had been this tremendous. This was the first time he had experienced such a level of pain, and it was real.

Immediately Sam let out a scream that was louder than any human had ever screamed before. Twice as loud in fact. It vibrated the concrete walls and forced the guards to cover their ears in pain. Sam fell to the ground and began to writhe from the sheer agony of having his leg ripped open by a .223 caliber bullet. It tore through his skin like a hot knife through butter and left a splattering of blood on the patchy gray concrete wall behind him. He had no idea what to do. There he was on the ground at the top of the flight of stairs, hands clutching a hole in his leg, rolling back and forth.

His teeth clenched powerfully as he began to groan in agony. Those groans seemed to be forcibly pushed out from behind those teeth causing little bits of spit to spray from the corners of his mouth. If there was ever a time in his life when Sam was his most vulnerable, this was it. He had no idea of how to process the situation. Only seconds ago he believed, with every fiber of his being, that he was in a dream. He was now having a true moment of realization.

It didn't take long for his mind to start cranking out calculations and seeing possible situations despite the massive amount of pain that was radiating through his body from his leg. He knew that he was about to be in some serious shit. The guards that came to greet him were not your average, run-of-the-mill, fat asses that usually don the disguise of an authority figure. No, these were professionals. He could tell by their posture before shooting him, that they knew what they were doing. It was almost as if they knew he was there. Like they were waiting for him. He needed to escape, but before Sam could rise to his feet, they had found their way back on to theirs. In the blink of an eye, they were on top of the stairs with rifles pointing down at his face. One placed his hand on his hip and depressed a button. It clearly triggered some kind of walkie-talkie.

"Target has been disabled. We are strapping him up and preparing to deliver the package to you, sir," said the soldier.

Obviously, his response was to someone on the other end of the radio. Sam should have been able to tune into the voice in the soldier's ear, but he was far too distracted by the pain in his leg and the multiple rifles in his face.

"You fucking shot me!!!! Mother fucker! I can't believe you shot me!" he said in a defiant and incredulous voice.

The soldiers that stood over him said not a word. They reached down and forcibly turned Sam over onto his stomach. Prying his arms behind him, they cinched up a wire tie around his wrists. All he could do was scream from the tremendously painful sensations flowing from his leg. He could already feel the blood beginning to pool underneath his shorts as it continued to soak the already stained clothes.

Today was turning out to be a very bad day.

Normally in a situation like this, Sam's first instinct would have been to cower. Give in to the authoritarian figure that was now hoisting him off the ground by the back of his neck. He would have followed along with the commands being given to him like "don't do anything stupid" and "just cooperate kid." However, today was anything but normal. Today, Sam was not himself. The shooting pain coming from his leg was not as intense as it was even moments ago. The armed guards treating him like a hardened criminal did not intimidate him. He was not prepared to do as they commanded. He was not going to go willingly.

Dropping his chin to his chest, he took in a deep breath. On the inhale, he assessed his situation. Five guards, one in front, one on each side, two behind. A piece of cake. Though his hands were still bound behind him, he knew he would be out of this situation in less than ten seconds. On the exhale, he tore through the zip tie that was binding his hands as if it were made of play dough.

In a single motion, he brought his hands up and gripped the back of the guards' necks that were on either side of him. In the same motion, he raised his right leg and delivered a chest shattering front kick to the guard in front of him. The kick, so well executed, it sent the guard flying down the stairs without touching a single step. He smashed into the wall some twenty feet away making a thud that sounded like a bag of potatoes.

Sam threw the guard in his left hand up into the concrete underside of the staircase above them. He too fell like a sack of potatoes.
Dragging the guard in his right hand across to the wall on his left, he rocketed the poor guard face first into the

concrete. Pieces of his face shield and helmet exploded into the air followed by blood and teeth. The guard on his back left grabbed Sam's shoulder as soon as he broke through the zip tie. But everything was happening so fast that he didn't even have time to pull his hand away before Sam grabbed it with the strength of a vice, crushing all the bones in an instant. The guard on his back right was caught completely off guard by all the action that exploded in front of him. He was barely able to make a move before he caught the full force of Sam's right elbow to his face. Again...potatoes against the wall.

Without relinquishing the guard's hand, he brought his right hand back around and with a slight pivot on his left foot; he delivered a devastating punch to the final guard's face. The guard flew backward and smashed into the wall without his arm. Sam quickly snapped back into a position of control and dominance. The twinge of pain overwhelmed him once again. His jaw tightened, and he began to feel the stirring of both pain and adrenaline coursing through his veins.

He dropped the severed arm.

"Six seconds," he said to himself.

Once again, he tuned his ears to see if anyone else was coming up the stairs. What he heard was rather disturbing. Amidst the sound of his breath and heart, he did not hear anything else. No other footsteps or clicking and clacking of gear. No breath was coming out from behind masks. No rustling of fabric.

No other heartbeats. Besides his own, he couldn't hear any at all; including the five men that lay motionless on the floor. No breath. No pulse. No motion.

For the first time in his life, Sam had taken life through a conscious decision of his own. His impulse reaction had cost these five men their lives.

"Five men," he thought aloud. Five husbands, five sons, five fathers. Five lives. Gone in six seconds. The force of Sam's blows was powerful enough to take lives, but the strength of his shame was enough to make him vomit...and then flee.

Chapter 12: Didn't See That Coming

More powerful than he had ever imagined himself to be, Sam rushed down the stairs in a completely panicked state. This slender young man, barely in his twenties had just killed five fully armed, grown men as if it were child's play. That is exactly how he felt, like a sniveling little child. The fact that he had just killed those men was the catalyst for a train of thoughts that would crush his mental well-being.

He treated them as if they were a minor obstacle in his way. Once he decided to act, they were dead before he even knew what he had done. This only reaffirmed what Michael had told him earlier. He was missing all of his memory from the night before. With all the blood staining his shirt and the rampage that he saw happening in his dream, maybe it was him. Maybe he did kill all those men.

"Oh God," he thought to himself.

He didn't want to be a monster. He had always wanted to have strength and power over the assholes in the world. To be able to give people their just deserts. But, not like this. He didn't want to kill people with a single punch, and he certainly didn't want to do it without any thought behind his actions.

Could he have handled that situation better? Did he have

to kill those guards? If only he had more control over what was happening to him. If he had some time to ease into it. Time to practice, maybe then he could do good with this power and not hurt anyone. However, the time for practice was over. Doing things the right way was an option that he did not have. Maybe he should have just listened to Michael instead of being so cocky and thinking he knew it was all a dream. If he had just taken a moment to shut his goddamned mouth those men might be alive and he might not have this gaping wound in his leg.

However, this was the price he was paying for not accepting reality. He thought about the consequences that he was going to have to pay. What happens when they catch him? He was too young to go to jail. He couldn't afford a lawyer.

Sam stopped dead in his tracks. He sat down on the step halfway down the flight. Dropping his face into his hands, Sam knew that if Frank were here, he would tell him to suck it up. He would say that there was no time to be a little bitch about it now; that they need to get out of there. But, that was a thought he didn't need to have. That one thought opened a floodgate of memory and emotion. His eyes welled up with tears at the realization that his friend was truly dead.

His chin wrinkled and quivered. The memories of what happened last night raced through his head like some science fiction movie flashback. He would never be able to see Frank again. His best friend was gone. What was he going to do? What was Frank's mother going to do? She was a single mother. Frank was all she had. He was all Sam had. He was the cool, calm and collected one. The one that kept Sam anchored. Frank taught Sam to be a good person. So what if he was a bit arrogant and stole a few things? At heart, he was a good person. He was kind and gracious. He would have taken a bullet for Sam.

And he did.

All Sam could do was sob uncontrollably. Eyes smashed forcibly into the heels of his hands; he let out all the heartache he had inside. It seemed far worse than he thought it should be. Maybe his feelings of sorrow and loss were doubled from what was happening to him. Maybe, he was just unprepared for the loss of the only person he ever considered his friend. Either way, it hurt deeply.

As he sat there, on those steps amidst the screaming sound of the alarm with tears streaming down his face, the memories of the previous evening flashed over him with perfect recollection.

There he stood, looking down at Frank. He could see in gory detail his best friend's body lying on that dank concrete slab. A giant pool of blood flowing outward from behind his head. The tiny hole in the front and the massive exit wound that was barely revealing itself. He watched Frank die in vivid, graphic detail and there was nothing he could do about it. He could not save him or bring him back. His friend was gone. Dead. The savagery he was forced to watch himself perform from a third person point of view was more than he could bear. All of those men. Dead. Slaughtered. And there was nothing he could do to change it.

Even though it was his hands ripping them to shreds, he felt as though he was not a part of the process. The feeling of helplessness was a feeling he knew all too well. It was like being trapped in The Furnaces and watching that thing that lived there torment him as it did for all those years. Sam wept like the child he had trapped deep inside and hid away all those years ago. He wept as though he were saying his last goodbyes to all those that ever meant anything to him. He knew what was waiting for him at the bottom of that staircase. Those men that he killed were not calling back on their radios. They were not answering their cell phones. Someone was about to find them. It was only a matter of time. Things were about to get very ugly. There would be lots cops. Lots of cameras. And lots of bullets.

If the authorities caught him, they would send him to jail for the rest of his life. Maybe even give him the death penalty, if they didn't kill him first. There was nothing he could do. The dream that he realized was a reality had turned into a living nightmare.

Sam took a few more minutes and began to choke back the tears. He was able to bring the sorrowful sobs down to the irregular breaths that come after a good hard cry. A couple of hard pulls through the nostrils to suck the snot back into his head, he realized he must look like a shamble of a human being. There he sat, covered in blood both from last night and the gunshot wound to his leg. He had spatters of blood from the men he had just violently killed. His eyes were bloodshot from the massive outpouring of tears. The parts of his skin and clothes that were not covered in blood were caked with dirt and sewer sludge. Sam had never been this low before. The evil that he experienced as a child was not even enough to bring him this far down. If he wasn't really in a dream, then this staircase was the road down to Hell.

What was awaiting him? He had taken notice of several cameras in the stairwell on the way down. He knew someone was watching. There was no way that he was walking out of this building consequence free. Someone would be coming after him. With the string of mass shootings that had been plaguing the country over the past few years, the police had adopted a military posture and the response time was swift. Without a doubt, they would be coming after him.

Tuning his ears in again, he could hear the movement of people. The faint chatter of radios. The sounds of accelerated heartbeats in the lobby just a few floors below him. There were large trucks pulling up outside and people stopping traffic. He could hear random people asking what was going on as they were ushered away from the building.
He wasn't going to walk out of this building. He either would be shot again or be arrested.

With one final suck of snot and a loud sigh, he rose to his feet as though the executioner was calling his name.

"Well," he said aloud "perfect end to the perfect fucking day."

He took one more deep, calming breath and began to take his first defeated step down the stairs in what was looking like a long journey to face some poorly orchestrated music. As his foot hit the stair below, it made a sound like thunder. That thunder came laced with a raspy voice that was all too familiar to him.

"You pathetic piece of shit." the voice thundered. "You are unworthy of such power."

The voice was the one from his nightmare. The one that he heard every night for years. It was like listening to James Earl Jones after twenty years of smoking six packs a day. The voice was reverberating through the concrete encased stairwell. Sam had never heard this voice in his waking life, only in his dreams. Nevertheless, there was no mistaking it. It was Malice. But why was he hearing it now?

He took another step.

"Such a weak thing has been given such a strong gift, and you have no idea how to use it," the voice rattled.

Sam said nothing in return as he tried to figure out if he

really heard the voice or just making himself hear it in a sort of mortification for his recently committed atrocities.

"You have never been so strong; yet, you feel guilty. Such greatness, wasted on such an imbecile. Give me the reigns and I will lay waste to them like I did before. You can cry as you watch me rip their flesh from their bones," proclaimed Malice.

Sam took a few quick steps to reach the landing below him and he threw a very hard kick into the wall in front of him, causing it to crack slightly. Balling his fists by his side, Sam belted out rather loudly, "FUCK YOU! GO AWAY!"

"I couldn't leave even if I wanted to and you cannot get rid of me," Said Malice. "I have tried to kill you for ages. Your weakness nauseates me as I am forced to watch the world through you."

Sam began to trot down the stairs a bit faster. His attitude began to shift ever so slightly from sorrow and sadness to a disposition of aggravation. He had struggled for years to get that voice out of his head. Now it was drowning out his thoughts.

"Do you think they are going to arrest you? They want to kill you. They almost did. If I hadn't saved you, they would've put you on your knees and then killed you," growled Malice from deep inside.

"I am not weak! I'm not. You are not real. You're just a voice in my head," Sam told him in a reaffirming manner, trying to convince himself that the voice was not real. Today, though, anything could be real.

"Then what will you do, scared little boy? Will you march to your own death? Or will you fight?"

"I can't fight. I don't want to kill anyone else."

"I can fight for you," Malice tempted Sam.

"I won't let you out again. I can't."

"You can...and you will. You don't have what it takes to stop me. I will wait until you are weak and I will put you in that box. Then I will kill everything around you," Threatened Malice.

"I control you!!!! You can't put me in that box. Not out here!!!!!!" Sam barked back.

His level of sorrow swiftly turned into full-blown pissed off. A defiant wave flowed over him as he took in a deep breath and changed his posture, chest up and shoulders back. The pain in his leg had all but vanished. He no longer wanted to give up. He had no desire to submit or simply accept the fate that he believed was in store for him. Malice's taunting had provoked a change in Sam's mentality. Sam began to solve the problem that was facing him. How to get out of this stairwell alive? How to escape?

Michael had told him that he was twice what any human was. He was faster, stronger and smarter. Why should he succumb to death? Why give himself over to power hungry jarheads that have more authority than they deserve? They don't know anything about him. They don't know how fast or how strong he is. Also, he was certainly more clever than they were.

Sam began to grin as he looked up the stairwell. He turned around and bolted back up the stairs he had just come down. Bounding up sets of stairs with a single step, it was only moments before he returned to the scene of his violent onslaught. There was the soldier. Still in the same position, he was in when Sam left him only moments ago.

Though he knew nothing would change, he still felt as though it was supposed to. Deep down inside, Sam was still clinging to the notion that this was still a dream. Sam had no more time to give to the men that he had killed. The instinct of survival had doubled in him, and he could do nothing to undo what had already been done. These men were dead, and there was no changing it.

Quickly but carefully, Sam darted over the bodies and around the pools of blood that coated the steps like spilled motor oil. He approached the exit door at the top of the stair set. Reading that this was the entrance to the ninth floor, he thought to himself that this would be just perfect. With a quick kick to the center of the door, he sent it flying out into the rows of cubicles that covered the floor.

Walking out into the office area, he felt awkward, out of place. The awkward you feel when you are in an elevator full of suits wearing only a Speedo and one sock. The smell of after-shave and cheap perfume wafted up into his nostrils. The putrid smell was already bad enough before the craziness of these new abilities set in. Now it was sickening. He would have to learn how to control this too.

Looking left and right to get a grip on his bearings, he saw what he was looking for, the east side of the building. In a brisk pace, he walked beyond the endless sea of empty cubicles and over to the window. Below was a nine-story drop onto the asphalt. If he somehow managed to survive, the fall there was a small army down there waiting to put a few bullets in him. He truthfully had no intentions of falling. Across from him sat another building covered in glass.

"Fifty-four feet and nine inches," He said to himself. "I can do that," Sam proclaimed with confidence.

Looking up, he could see the three snipers on the roof waiting for the chance to put a bullet in him. As the lens flare of a sniper's scope caught his attention, he could practically smell the laser dots that were wiggling around on his forehead. This was going to be tricky.

As Sam backed away from the window, the

computations began rattling off in his head. Trajectory and force, impact and air resistance. Everything he thought he knew nothing about. Michael had mentioned that he wouldn't just instantly know new things, so he was slightly surprised by this sudden flood of knowledge crashing into his brain. Nevertheless, he didn't have time to question it. He knew the math was right, and this was the only way out.

All Sam needed now were filing cabinets. Looking around, he saw that there were quite a few to choose from. This office was full of cubicles, and he could have his pick. He walked up to the closest group of them, and he was in luck; two of them that were the same size. Large, slightly off white and they appeared to be just heavy enough. He smashed his hands down on the corners of them crushing in the flimsy metal to get a firm grip. For some reason, being able to crumple the metal in his hands put a small but ever so satisfying grin on his face.

Sam turned and pulled the two filing cabinets behind him. As he drew closer to the window, he began to build up a tremendous amount of speed. Just feet from the window, he flung both filling cabinets with remarkable velocity, one after the other, through the thick plates of glass. Thousands of shards of glass and stacks of paper flew out the window, and Sam followed out behind them with a powerful leap. The thought that ran through his head was, "God, let this work." but the words that seeped from his lips were, "Try this on for size fuckers."

The glass and paper served as a great distraction for those below that would attempt to shoot him. Every person beneath him was busy taking cover from the falling glass or trying to distinguish Sam from the paper fluttering through the sky. The snipers on the roof were having the same problem, but Sam had counted on them being a bit sharper than that. The two large filing cabinets that were flying out in front of him would act as shields to guard him, should one of the snipers attempt a blind shot hoping to get lucky.

Sam pulled this plan out of his ass, and it seemed to be working. His intelligence was beginning to show. He started to hear the pings and dings of bullets hitting the filing cabinets along with the whizzing of bullets flying past him from very haphazardly fired shots coming from the ground. All of this was happening in the blink of an eye, Sam's ability to process everything going on around him made it feel like an eternity.

His brain was in overdrive counting the number of pieces of broken glass that were flying around him. One thousand five hundred and thirty-four, if you counted all of them, including the tiny little shards that were smaller than the tip of a ballpoint pen. He was also calculating the direction and angle of every bullet fired at him. He knew he was not going to get hit and that his plan was working quite well.

As he came to the realization that he was going to make it across the street, through the glass window of the other building, he was struck by the ramifications of his hastily approved plans and calculations. He had not taken into account that he had to land. And currently, he was traveling at 42 miles per hour, towards a glass-covered building, chasing two metal boxes, with no idea of what lay on the other side of the reflective black glass.

There was nothing that could be done about it now. The only thing left was to let gravity run its course and hope for the best. With the thunderous crash of glass and sheet metal, the world seemed to speed up as quickly as it slowed down. Sam and the two filing cabinets broke through the glass and tumbled across the floor of yet another field of cubicles sending, even more, paper stirring through the air.

As soon as his body stopped rolling like a rag doll across the carpet covered floor he did a quick systems check on himself: thirteen bruises and scrapes, minor muscle damage and two friction burns, all of which were already beginning to repair themselves at accelerated rates. Beyond the few bangs and bruises, he was in otherwise great condition.

"No time to hang out here," he said to himself.

His ears lit up with the sound of radios full of disbelief and officers barking orders to grunts that were both amazed and scared shitless at the same time. He could see the red dots of lasers searching for something to shoot. They would waste no time coming after him. He needed to find a way out and fast. The authorities were already beginning to rush the stairwells and elevators. That meant the only way out was the same way he came in. Sam turned around and started running toward the other side of the giant office. He had already calculated the speed, distance, and angle for his exit. Now the only thing left was to break the glass. A swift soccer style kick to a trash can solved the problem. Just like before he exploded out of the building in a shower of glass.

Before last night in the sewer, Sam would have needed to roll to get rid of this much energy when landing. But today, a parked car provided all the cushion he needed. Lucky for him, there was one right below him.

The people that were standing on the street behind the police barricades were not as lucky. Sam crashed down on the car's roof. Its windows exploded outward with ferocious force, slicing open dozens of innocent people. He stood up on the roof of the crumpled vehicle only to see them screaming and covering their wounds. Others were staring at him trying to figure out what was going on. It was only a second before the screaming turned into a panic.

Sam's actions had caused even more people to be in pain. He never thought that he would hurt anybody else while trying to save his own sorry ass.
A wave of remorse swept over him for the pain that he had just caused. Perhaps more remorse than anyone else would have in this situation. It was an accident, but it was an accident brought on by his actions. He did not want to hurt them; but, he had no time to stick around

and help them. While he felt such an overwhelming need to rectify his mistake, his desire for self-preservation was far greater. He knew those soldiers would be there in just a few moments. These people would get the medical care they needed. Though he felt tremendous guilt, there was nothing he could do for them right now.

He could hear the sirens and soldiers just around the corner. He knew they were going to shoot to kill. He knew that if he stayed here, more people could get hurt. He couldn't risk any more innocent people getting injured. As his heart filled with anxiety and his teeth clenched with adrenaline, his mind began to fill with questions. Why was this happening? Would he get to see this Michael character again? Would he see Julia again?
There was only one question that needed answering right this moment. How fast could he run?

Chapter 13: Run Like Hell

A swelling of energy gathered in Sam's quads and calves. The need to explode into a flat out sprint was clear. His life depended on it. He needed to vanish. One would naturally assume that since he practiced parkour that he would be able to run like the wind, but parkour was an art of explosive power and not true speed and distance. Yesterday, Sam would have been winded after fifty yards of a full sprint. Today, however, was not yesterday. Many things Sam had done today were miraculously different from yesterday. He was ready to see what his legs had in store for him today.

Within the first few steps, he could tell the difference. There was not going to be any disappointments in his legs today. His strides were long and powerful. He was covering large swaths of ground with every step. The interchange of energy spent and force returned was phenomenal. It was faster than he had ever moved before, and he was not even at full speed. The bullet wound to his leg was barely even noticeable at this point. He didn't know if it had healed itself or if it was because of adrenaline and endorphins.

Tearing down the center of the crowded city street, he was covering the length of a block in less time than it took to breath in a full lung of air. The sound of the wind whipping past his ears was deafening. There is a point when the power of this kind of sprinting leaves the body, and the muscles and lungs can no longer keep up. That point showed absolutely no signs of being anywhere close. He was running a flat out full sprint, and his body was repairing fatigued muscles on the fly.

Sam had a bit of giddiness building in the back of his mind. The experience of this kind of speed had to be one of the coolest things that had happened to him today, right next to the whole jumping across a city street while avoiding snipers thing. However, the excitement would have to wait. The rhythmic thump of helicopters blades at low levels was not far behind him. As long as they could see him, they could track him. If he were going to escape, he would need cover away from the helicopters. He needed to be in a place that was familiar. A place that he knew every nook and cranny. That place was his neighborhood, Hipsterville.

If he were there, he could find lots of cover. He knew every square inch of that place from all the countless days of training. There was not a single nook or cranny that he couldn't find. If he were there, no one would find him.

He would have a chance to think. A chance to breathe. A chance to figure things out. The problem with Hipsterville, it was back the other way, across the bridge. It was the only bridge that cut across the river for miles. That meant going back through the mess that he was running away from.

He put on the brakes and stopped running. The rush of air that he had created in his mad dash through the city streets caught up with and blew past him. There was no sense in running any further in the opposite direction. Home was the right decision, and he knew it. But going home would only offer a reprieve. There was no real escape from these soldiers, and he knew it.

He couldn't help but think that these guys knew who he was. He came down into the tower that Michael dropped him on, and they were there, waiting. Were they tracking him since last night? Surely not. If that were the case, they would have nabbed him in his sleep. There were pieces of this puzzle that didn't fit. Nevertheless, he would have to go somewhere other than his house. Some place safe. Some place like Julia's apartment. The journey there was going to be a tough one.

"This is about to be the dumbest move I have ever made," Sam said as a peculiar sign of reassurance to himself.

He knew this was about to be a hell of a run. It was three miles away to the very edge of his neighborhood. Then another ten blocks of left and right turns, through the poorly laid out streets. Lucky for him, he knew the way through the back alleys.

The thumping of the helicopter was drawing to a stop directly overhead now. The whipping blades drove the air down onto the ground and kicked up dust. It stung his eyes and blew his clothes around. Pulling his forearm in front of his face as a feeble attempt to guard himself against all the blowing dirt and dust, he looked up at the mechanical monstrosity. The side door started to slide open. Sam knew what was next. He needed to start running, or he would be shot. Any second a man was going to pop out of that door and put any number of bullets in him. There were hundreds of action films stashed away in his memory banks to remind him that he was not safe.

"Well shit, here we go," Sam said and then took off like a bat out of Hell.

Pushing himself to full sprint as fast as possible, he knew it would only take a few seconds before running into the dozens of heavily armed men that were trying to kill him just moments earlier. Maybe he would get lucky enough to blow right past them. Though the likelihood of that was slim considering, there was a helicopter chasing him. He also knew no matter how fast he ran; he couldn't outrun a radio. But that didn't mean that he wasn't about to try.

As the blocks zipped past, the wind got quieter. He could feel his senses starting to dial themselves in. He was able to pattern his breathing and calm the adrenaline rush that had possessed him thus far. He could see the men on the horizon with clear accuracy. Even though they were just outside of the normal person's range of vision, he could count them. Moreover, he could sense them. He could smell them.

He didn't smell them with his nose, per say. He didn't smell their body odor. It was as if he could smell their intent. Some had the intent to kill driven by fear. Others had the intent to stay alive driven by fear. One among them felt different. It was as if he had felt it before. There was a strange feeling of connection. It was like the feeling he got from the soldier in the cave that Malice spared. Something told him they were the same person.

The closer he got, the stronger these feelings got. He could sense the fingers quivering on triggers. He could feel the anxiousness coming from the mass of men and metal. Was this what all men in war felt? How nerve-racking it must be to be a soldier. Sam did not envy them.

He knew that a head-on approach would get him killed. He needed to detour and get a head start on them before they were able to chase him. He would have the advantage if he played it right. His knowledge of the city was vast, and he was quite fast at the moment. That large amount of people and vehicles would take a moment to mobilize again. The helicopter above him was going to be a problem, though. Everywhere he went, that damn thing was going to follow him.

What to do? He did not want to hurt anybody, but he was going to need a huge distraction to get out of this. He needed to slow down for a minute and analyze the situation. What could he use to his advantage? Sam stopped suddenly. His eyes raced back and forth, looking at everything around him. The cars, the street signs, the lights, everything. He looked to his right and saw a car parked there. He looked at the men that were around sixty yards away. They had conveniently gathered next to a fire hydrant and under a stop light. He felt the wind from the helicopter's blades pulsing above him. He instantly had a plan. Whether it would work or not remained to be seen.

Taking in a deep breath and then darting to the car on his right, he smashed his hand through the glass of the rear driver's side door, crushing the metal and the cheap plastic in his grip. In one seamless move, Sam ripped the door from the car with all of his might and flung it like a Frisbee down the street. The door smashed into the fire hydrant with remarkable force causing it to rupture and sending a massive stream of water spewing into the crowd of soldiers. It was just enough of a disruption to give him a way through.

Ripping the front door off, he flung it down range as well and struck the light post at its base causing it to crumble and fall into the men. Without missing a single step, Sam whipped around to the front of the car and stripped the car of its hood revealing the engine. With a quick spin, he threw the lightweight piece of formed sheet metal upwards at the helicopter. It reached incredible speeds as it traveled in a direct line towards its target. The pilot was able to avoid taking a direct hit, but the hood smashed into the propellers with a sound that caused Sam to cringe.

The helicopter began to spin out of control instantly as Sam's eyes popped wide open. It was most certainly an "OH SHIT" moment. The helicopter smashed into the building next to it and promptly fell to the ground sending shards of glass, metal, and asphalt flying in all directions. For a man that did not want to hurt anyone, he was failing miserably.
Now he was committed to his plan. Though injury and death were not part of it, Sam had caused both. But at that moment, he could not let either of those things distract him. Mourn later, run now.

Stepping backward with a few skips, he picked up the pace and began to sprint at full speed in between the buildings using alleyways and zig-zagging in between city blocks. A few tears streamed from his face as the responsibility of hurting those people got to him. The thought of all the people he had wounded or killed weighed in his stomach like a lead brick. The feeling of helplessness and not being in control were reminiscent of the days when he was a dog under the thumb of his parents. He did not have control then, and he sure didn't have control now. He hated not knowing what to do.

After blasting through a couple of miles of city streets, Sam was only a few blocks from his neighborhood. The only thing left now was to make it across the bridge. Just a short distance and he could vanish into some little hole in the wall. Salvation was so close, and yet, there was still no real way out of this mess.

The confidence that this massive increase in ability and power brought was coupled with a tremendous amount of remorse and sorrow. With one negative thought, he launched his self-doubt into a full-scale assault on his psyche. Today was turning out to be the worst kind of nightmare. One in which he was so lucid and yet so helpless in this environment.

"I just wanna wake up," he mumbled in a voice broken by the sorrow of the day.

But how could he wake up from a dream that was a reality? Today was quickly becoming more than he could handle again. His mood was vastly out of control along with his power. Sam was turning into a superior being, or so he was told. But he could not control his emotions. They swayed like leaves in the wind. First filling him with power and confidence, then with self-loathing and regret. He hated this. Just like clockwork when doubt entered his mind….so did the voice inside of his head

"Look at you running like a bitch," Malice said. "You don't deserve this power."

"Shut up!!!" Sam screamed as he came to a dead stop.

The wind created in his race across the city flew past him once again, rustling his hair and clothes.

"I am not going anywhere, Sam. The stronger you get, the stronger I get. The weaker you become, the sooner I am going to put you in that box and show you what we are really capable of," growled Malice's voice.

Sam clutched the side of his head and screamed so loud it rattled the windows in the surrounding buildings and vibrated the doors on their hinges. Falling to his knees, he punched the asphalt, cracking it like a flimsy dinner plate.

"You are weak, boy. So pathetic."

Sam could hear Malice as if it were standing next to him shouting right in his ear. He tried to tune the monster out, but there was no salvation for the troubled young man. What could he do? He had nowhere to go, no one that knew what was going on with him. He had no one to help him.

"I am all alone," he thought to himself. This sobering thought bled from his heart with passion and intent. It echoed in his mind so loudly that it drowned Malice out, if only for a moment.

Sam, however, was not alone. His statement of despair was powerful enough to act as a beckoning call. He felt a massive rush of air blasting at him the front. Without looking, he assumed another helicopter was hovering above him. Sam slowly lifted up his head to see a sight that surely must have been from Heaven.

There was Michael in all of his glory hovering above him, with wings of energy, not feathers, beating in massive, powerful strokes. Michael was bathed in a warm, penetrating light, the likes of which Sam had never seen. Even Michael's skin was drenched in this magnificent display of luminance. He spoke with a voice like thunder.

"You are never alone Sam Rittenhouse. I will be with you until the day that you die for the last time. But this thing that you carry with you must be silent!"

Michael placed his palm on Sam's forehead and began to murmur in words that Sam could not understand. Malice started to shriek and scream in resistance and agony. Michael's face grew stern as a scowl stretched itself around his now pitch black eyes.

In a tone that matched that of Malice's he said, "I command you back into the darkness, Malice. I refuse to hear thy voice. Twister of words be silent, or I will smite thee!"

Sam's face grimaced with pain. Whatever was going on inside him was not pleasant, and it seemed to resist this with all of its might. Sam simply could not believe that Michael was truly talking to Malice. He was nothing more than the boogieman in Sam's dreams. Could this be the voice that was tormenting him?

A deep growl came from inside Sam that did not resonate from his vocal cords. It erupted from a place inside where his gut was supposed to be, but he could only feel a hole in its place. Then the growl was gone.

"I can see your wings, Michael," Sam said. The words could barely tumble from his lips. The exhaustion of the day was catching up with him.

"There are lots of things you can see now Sam." I will tell you about all of them, but we have to leave now. Those poorly dressed men and their silly little guns are coming, and I can't have you dying again just yet."

Michael scooped Sam up, offering support to the young man who had gone through so much today.

Sam looked at Michael and said, "This sucks!"

"You don't know the half of it. Let's get a drink before it gets worse… shall we?"

Michael thrust his wings. With a single beat, they were gone.

Chapter 14: The Truth of it All

Michael had flown them far outside of the city. The events of the day rested on Sam's head like a ton of bricks as the two descended through the trees to the leaf covered ground. Neither one of them said a word since they took off. It wasn't an uncomfortable silence, though. Michael was giving Sam time to cope with what was going on, and Sam was using that time wisely. He needed to replay all of these events and try to make sense of everything. There were simply too many unanswered questions.

"What is going on with me?" Sam solemnly asked.

"I suppose you are due for a proper answer," Michael replied as he turned his head to avoid eye contact.

"Listen, I am sorry I had to leave you in a situation like that, but my orders were to show you what you were capable of, and I couldn't think of a better way to do it than to let you spread your wings a bit."

Sam said nothing, his gaze fell to the ground, and the hollow appearance of self-disgust filled his eyes.

"Ah...I know what's got you. The people you killed, it bothers you, right?" Michael had seen this face before. "Yeah, Ismael was like that too in the beginning. Listen, you have killed a few people in the past twenty-four hours. By average standards, that makes you a very effective mass murderer. But, these are not average circumstances. These people are sheep. They live meaningless lives and walk around pondering their existence so much that they miss the life that is happening right in front of them!" Michael passionately proclaimed

"But you…you are the first person to experience this in over 5000 years. You're not like everybody else," said Michael.

"Yeah, that's pretty fucking apparent. Most people don't knock helicopters out of the fucking sky with the hood of a goddamn car!" rattled Sam in his sarcastic voice. "What you still haven't told me is what is happening to me and why."

"Why is easier than what…so let's start there," shrugged Michael.

"Fucking finally!" exclaimed Sam.

"You are this way because of a flower." said Michael.

Sam clenched his fist and tightened his jaw. The irritation raced through him faster than his blood. He flung his arm out to the side and smacked a tree with the side of his fist so hard that the trunk shattered and the small tree came crashing down.

"You wanted answers? That was one of those answers. I

am more than happy to answer any questions you have. But I am just telling you right now, you might not like the answers I give you. I have all the time in the world to wait for you to calm down before I give them to you," Michael proclaimed with authority.

The look on Michael's face was in direct defiance of the hotheaded young man that stood before him. His lips drew back and his eyebrows raised as if to challenge Sam to overcome his anger.

"You just said that this is happening to me because of a flower...how the fuck do you expect me to react?" asked Sam.

"I will never lie to you Sam, but there are times when I am going to have to tell you things you don't want to hear. So if you can just calm down for a moment we can get down to business, and I can fill you in on everything you need to know," said Michael.

"Alright then..." Sam sat down and leaned his back against a tree ".... shoot."

"I was very serious when I said this is happening to you because of a flower. The one, you and Frank, tried to steal last night, it was not just an average, ordinary flower. That flower only grows when a God has been absent from this world for 100 years. Only one person on the planet can pull that flower from the ground. Only one person can bond with it. That one person is you."

"Bullshit!" Sam proclaimed, "I didn't bond with a damn thing."

"You were shot directly in the head, your blood got on the flower, and you bonded with it. You don't remember because technically, you were dead."

"Dead?" questioned Sam

"Yeah, dead. The process didn't happen the way it was intended. First, you make the bond, and then you max out, and then you die. But no, you had to take the fast way and die right out of the gates."

"I am so confused. Max out?" Sam questioned with a bewildered look on his face.

"OK. So first, when your blood touched the flower it made a bond with you on a DNA level. You were supposed to be alive when that bond was made. When you bond, the flower alters you on an atomic level. Don't ask…we don't know how. Second, when that alteration happens, it makes you into the perfect specimen of a human. You are as strong as any human could ever be. Your eyesight is as good as it could ever get. Same for your hearing, taste, touch, smell, reflexes, immunities, etc. If it is something the human body does, you could have done it better than any other human on the planet. However, those improvements stretch far beyond just the physical; they also include the mental, emotional and spiritual. Given enough time, you could have made the most intelligent scientist look like a babbling idiot, and dwarfed the Dali Lama in the understanding of the spiritual self," explained Michael.

"This would have been the perfect opportunity for you to become adjusted to this new state of existence as well as learn to control it. It would have prepared you for the falling of the first petal. And it would have been a more manageable transition."

"So what went wrong?" asked Sam

"You got shot in the head...then you made the bond. The flower immediately brought you back to life, and you bypassed the first ascension in seconds, where it should have taken several hundred years."

"So let me get this straight, I died...and the flower brought me back to life. Now I am some super human that missed 200 years of training...and I can throw cars." In a very Ted Theodore Logan fashion, Sam cocked his head slightly to the side and said, "Whoa."

"Yeah, this rabbit hole goes a lot deeper than that. There are two reasons you went berserk and turned that cavern into a slaughterhouse last night. This resurrection process has a built-in defense mechanism. Each time the flower brings you back to life, it ramps up your abilities to about four times what you were before you died."

"Why does it do that?" Sam asked

"So you can kill what killed you. Simple math when you

think about it. The second reason is something far more sinister. I haven't figured out what to make of it."

"What's that?" asked Sam

"Malice," said Michael with a solemn tone. "That is one sinister bastard you've got in there. I hate to see what he is going to be like on the next ascension."

"The next ascension? You mean this is going to happen again?" Sam questioned.

"Oh yeah. No doubt about that. Eleven more times to be exact." professed Michael. "Your flower had twelve petals on it. You have eleven left. Each time you die the flower will resurrect you and double what you were before. Your power is far greater than what it is supposed to be, though."

"Fuck me. What's the point in all that?"

"The point is for you to replace God. Plain and simple," Michael said as bluntly as possible.

"I think I need a second to process all this."

Sam placed his face into the palm of his hands and began to rub his stress out. It was a very heavy concept. Replacing God? Ascending? A magic flower that brings him back to life? The absurdity of it all would almost be humorous if he hadn't experienced everything he had today. This was certainly not the answer he was hoping for. But beneath the enormity of this entire situation was one simple fact that he had to accept, he was going to become a god, and that was pretty god damned cool. He pulled his face from his hands and asked, "Eleven times you say? How long is that gonna take?"

"It took Ismael four thousand years."

"FOUR THOUSAND YEARS??????" Sam was not expecting an answer like that.

"When the only thing they have to kill you with is sticks, swords, and stones it takes a while. But judging by how he looks now, I imagine he found a way to die a few times in the past hundred years."

Sam's eyes opened as wide as they could be. He had officially had enough up to this point. Though he was not physically fatigued anymore, his mind and soul had taken more than they could handle. The day had worn through his thin exterior of a soul. Death, destruction, surprise, violence and mayhem had followed him at every step. If this was going to be the normal, he was going to need to prepare. He just needed a bit of time to catch his breath.

Mostly, he needed a shower and a change of clothes. Sam was still wearing the blood-soaked clothes he had woken in this morning. He was still caked in the remains of the men he had killed in the stairway. He could still smell the stench of the sewer he and Frank had tromped through the night before. The stress of all the running and killing was permeating through the pores of his skin. Sam had never felt this dirty before.

Honestly, he could have stayed in the woods all day. At least, no one was trying to kill him there. There were no helicopters trying to take him out. No snipers or men dressed in full tactical armor. He could smell the fresh air and hear things he had never heard before. All the plants had a new texture. Even the simple beauty of the dirt and dead leaves underneath him was enough to calm him slightly.

This wasn't going to last, and he knew it. He couldn't count on anything being the way it was before. At the very least, he was going to be wanted for murder. If this God thing was anywhere near as heavy as Michael made it out to be, he was in for a long ride. Might as well figure out how it all works.

"I need a burger and beer," Sam said.

"I don't believe you have made a truer statement all day."

"You fly, I'll buy." said Sam.

"Deal."

Chapter 15: Meanwhile

The police had lent themselves to assist in the effort to track down the mysterious man that had gone on two rampages downtown. The amount of destruction that had been brought on by one man was simply astonishing and had elevated the presence of the military, as well as a private security force that was on loan to the US government by the Cain corporation. Both parties had taken over the police station as sort of a makeshift war room.

Dr. Wallace, Sam's former therapist, sat in a chair at the end of a small oak conference table with four very stern looking generals staring at him expecting an answer. The room was also made a bit more intense by a younger looking gentleman standing in the corner in a very sharp suit with a lack of expression on his face. Dr. Wallace was at a complete loss for words. His expression was one of awe as he viewed the security camera footage from the street and various other bits of footage the military and Cain forces had gathered. He knew what he was looking at couldn't be real. Humans can't do this sort of thing. But the deadly serious looks on everyone's faces in the room lead him to believe that the footage was genuine. Finally, one of the several generals broke the silence.

"Do you recognize the young man in that video?"

"I do indeed. That is Sam Rittenhouse. He is…. was a patient of mine," said Dr. Wallace as he readjusted himself in the fake leather office chair. Another general piped up.

"We are going to need you to tell us everything you can about Mr. Rittenhouse, Dr. Wallace."

"I am afraid I can't do that. It would be in direct conflict with doctor-patient confidentiality."

An apparent shake came over his hands as he fidgeted with his glasses. He had never had to pull that kind of a card with this many ominously serious people in the room. He knew it was a weak play considering the footage he had just seen, but it was worth a shot if nothing else.

"Dr. Wallace, Sam Rittenhouse has killed over 30 men in the past 24 hours. I don't care about your damn oath as a doctor. What I do care about is stopping this monster before he kills anyone else," barked the general. "You can cooperate, or I will have you thrown in a concrete hole for the next 20 years for aiding a terrorist and violating the Patriot Act."

Dr. Wallace became even more visibly shaken after the general's stern and aggressive threat. It was without a doubt the most aggression he had ever experienced from someone towards him that was not a patient.

"Easy General, no need to carry this too far." the doctor

stated in a voice that wreaked of self-preservation "I will cooperate. Just tell me what you want to know."

Dr. Wallace wasn't a cowardly man, but he wasn't stupid either. They were going to get what they wanted out of him no matter what. No sense in making his life uncomfortable.

"Let's start with any medical diagnoses you've made on him," chimed in another of the generals.

"I could write a book on Sam, gentlemen. He was a very deeply troubled young man. His official diagnosis was that he suffered from severe schizophrenia, as well as dissociative identity disorder. He never really got violent, but he did have some very rough times."

"Doctor, could you translate that into English for us, please. We are soldiers, not scholars."

"Certainly, General. Sam came from a very abusive home. He was treated very poorly from the day he was born. His parents didn't have the slightest clue that he was having issues, and frankly, they didn't care. It could have been a minor issue, but it grew with time. In fact, it became something quite serious. Sam hears a voice in his head. That voice is incredibly vile to him. It tells him that he is a horrible person in some of the worst ways possible. Sam was in a constant battle to suppress this voice all day, every day. To further complicate the matter, the voice would often become too strong for him to suppress and would eventually take over his psyche," explained the doctor.

"So we have a nut case on our hands?"

"No, you don't. Sam is a very capable human being. For the most part, he is smarter than your average Joe. However, this other persona that lives in his subconscious is a very violent and destructive side of Sam. It calls itself Malice. That thing in those videos, that's not Sam. That is Malice."

"If we are going to be able to get at this guy, we are going to need more info. What triggers his anger? What are some personal connections that he might have?" questioned one of the other Generals.

"Any number of things can trigger his anger. He was always a bit of a bombshell when we were dealing with Malice. Anytime Sam felt like he was being attacked Malice would step in and take over. It's almost as if Malice was his protector and tormentor at the same time. Malice viewed Sam as weak and yearned to be in control."

"What stopped him?" asked the man in the corner as he stepped forward.

"I'm sorry, exactly who are you?" asked the doctor.

"My name is Cain. Earlier today, Sam broke into my building, killed several of my men and destroyed one of my helicopters. He also trespassed on my property last night and destroyed a very important piece of research that my company has been working on for the past twenty years. I am very much involved in this manhunt, so...if you don't mind...what stopped him?"

Cain brought a very cold presence into the conversation. He was an average sized man with very dark skin. Dr. Wallace couldn't quite place his origin, but he had a very Middle Eastern look to him. His face was very young, but the streaks of gray in his beard and hair gave him an air of wisdom and age that was very striking. His confidence and mannerisms made him appear to be the type of person the doctor cared not to trifle with.

"Nothing. We tried everything. Hypnosis, breathing, sedation, restraints. None of it worked. Time was the only thing that would do the trick. We just had to let him calm down on his own," explained the doctor.

"What about family and friends?" asked another general.

"I haven't seen Sam since his mother and father were killed in a fire. I know nothing about his friends currently. However, when he was in sessions with me he often spoke of a friend named Frank. I am terribly sorry, but I don't know his last name."

"We do," said the final general at the table.

He opened a manila folder that was laying on the table in front of him. He slid a picture of Franks dead body across the table at the doctor.

"That is Frank" the general stated with confidence. "He died last night not too far from here."

"Is that a bullet hole in his head general?" asked the doctor.

"The details of Frank Saunters death have been classified, Dr. Wallace. Truth be told, we need any information that you can give us to stop more innocent people from dying."

"I am afraid there isn't much I can help you gentlemen with. I will say this, though, if you are confronting Sam, and you use force, he will retaliate with force. If you anger him, you run the risk of unleashing Malice. If what I saw on those videotapes is any indication of what he is capable of, releasing that monstrosity is probably the last thing you want to do."

"Thank you for your time doctor, please see my assistant on the way out," said Cain.

As the doctor left the room and the door closed behind him, the conversation took a very dark turn.

"I am not quite sure I know what to say, Mr. Cain," said one of the generals. "When we agreed to this little experiment of yours, it was to see if we could splice the abilities of that flower into the DNA of soldiers. But what happened last night was both a phenomenal success and a colossal blunder at the same time."

Another of the generals chimed in, "The power that that young man displayed was far beyond anything ever seen by anyone in this room. But I don't remember clearing any human trials and I damn sure didn't clear the deaths of those soldiers down in that damn hole," he barked.

"Gentlemen," said Cain in the most confident ass-kissing voice possible. "this was not a test. We had no idea that these young men were going to break in last night. Let alone that they would even know where it was, or even that there was anything in there. They obviously had insight into what it was and how to get it. I am willing to bet that they were tipped off by one of the soldiers that you placed in the test site."

A third general leaped out of his chair and barked, "Are you suggesting that one of those soldiers was committing treason? Those were DAMN fine men that we assigned down in that pit, and now we are going to be giving flags to their mothers and wives! You pompous son of a bitch!"

Cain could practically see the steam rising from the general's head.

"It was merely a suggestion to explain the impossible. I truly have no idea how they knew what was going on. I have had a team of my top minds down there all night trying to figure out exactly how he was able to do what he did."

"I think I speak for all of us when I say that I would like to see the test site and get a look at it myself. Also, I can't believe that this guy is a total hermit. He's got to have some family or friends. Maybe a romantic interest? Let's get everything we can from the NSA and track down a point of contact," one of the generals stated. "Wasn't there a soldier that survived this bloodbath intact? Let's get him front and center to answer a few questions."

Cain cleared his throat a took a moment to compose himself. It was apparent he was repressing his true response. These generals were important to his research and his company's geopolitical standing. Composure was of the upmost importance.

"We can most certainly visit the site. I will have a car meet you downstairs. I will need to change my clothes. This suit was quite expensive, and the site is less than acceptable for this ensemble."

Cain casually excused himself from the room and breathed a slight sigh of relief as the door closed behind him. He didn't care about the suit he was wearing. He had enough money to burn a five thousand dollar suit every day for the next hundred years and not see a dent in his bank account. He needed to move his people out and make sure that the site was still as intact as possible. He was elated at the course that the conversation had taken. He needed the military to accelerate the process. Sam was not quite up to the standards that he was hoping for. The young man that went on a high-speed chase through the streets was far from what he expected. Sam was going to need a bit more encouragement and nothing says encouragement like a soldier with a gun.

Chapter 16: A Beer, A Burger and A Story

As much of a snob as Michael was, when it came to good alcohol he knew that the best place to get a beer and a burger was a dive bar. He knew that the paramount place in this city was Gruffalo's. He didn't need special powers of divine intellect to find this out, just Google, the true compendium of the world's most useless knowledge. It was a close rival to his own knowledge. But the truth was that his knowledge was far more important and accurate.

Sam was eating like the monster he had become. Three burgers, four beers, a massive order of fries and he was just getting started. The trouble with having double everything is that he had double the appetite as well.

"I know that we have established that you are an angel, but what exactly is an angel? Not to be rude, but since we are going to be seeing a lot of each other, I assume, I think it's an important discussion to have," Sam asked.

"It's not rude. It's a very important question and has a great deal to do with why you are…" Michael pointed a french fry at Sam and waved it around "...what you are."

Setting his burger down and picking his napkin up off his lap, he wiped the little bits of mayo from the corner of his lips.

"Technically, I am not an angel. It is a clever title that Ismael gave us to help scare the shit out of people that he needed something from."

"You said 'us.' There are more of you?" asked Sam.

"There used to be. Now I am one of only three. I have been alive for eleven thousand years...and some change. I don't know much about where I came from, how I was made, or who made me. I... We were gifts to Ra..."

"The Egyptian sun god...The Ra?" Sam interrupted.

"The one and only. He didn't know much about who made us either, at least not in the beginning. All I remember is waking up on the ground beside dozens of other angels. Forty-two to be exact," Michael pulled a very tall and half gone beer up to his lips and proceeded to take a hard pull.

"We were his guardians at first, but after a few ascensions he didn't need us to protect him anymore. Then came the Egyptians. First they were just some small tribes that settled on the Nile. Those tribes turned to villages, villages to cities and so on. We steered clear of them and they had no idea we existed...until Ra got bored. He decided that the only way he was going to be able to ascend was if something stronger than him killed him."

"Wait he wanted someone to kill him?" questioned Sam.

People had tried to kill him several times today and it was not something that he enjoyed.

"Wait a couple thousand years and let's see how bored you get. Of course, it is slightly different for you. The monkeys are actually getting pretty smart these days. When Ra was walking the earth, they didn't even have the wheel." Michael took another swig of his beer and continued, "Anyway, he charged six angels with killing him. At this point it was no easy task and he decided to fight back to make the whole thing interesting. It was probably one of the most amazing battles I have ever seen. This thing went on for weeks. In the end they wound up killing him. Then he came back stronger and slaughtered them. That was when everything changed. We knew that if Ra was willing to slaughter six of us for his own amusement, he would have no problems killing the rest of us, me included."

Sam put down his burger, "I thought you couldn't die?"

"That comes later Sam, eat your burger and stop interrupting me. This is a fabulous story and I haven't been able to tell it to anyone for several millennia."

Michael continued, "People from all over Egypt saw this incredible battle. They told stories about it to each other. As they tried to make sense of it, the stories became more and more like the stories you would hear in a religious scripture. Thus, the Egyptian gods were born. Ra loved it. He took hold of the God identity and ran with it. He would make these grand appearances before the people so that they would further tell tales about him. Then as all things involving the ego do, it got worse."

Michael shoved another fry into his mouth and kept talking, "He started murdering people by the thousands. He would spend days meticulously torturing entire towns for fun. Immortality had taken its toll on him. We approached him and pleaded with him to control himself, but in response, he attacked us. As a group, we were able to hold him off, but Ra was no fool. Knowing that none of us could kill him, he could only think of one way to become stronger. He flew into the sun."

"Why didn't he just kill himself. Cut off his own head or something?" Sam asked.

"The flower wouldn't let him. He tried on many occasions to commit suicide to end his eternal boredom. Each time he tried, he failed." explained Michael.

"So why did flying into the sun work? Isn't that like suicide?"

"The sun is a star with incredibly strong gravity. Once he got too close, there was no way to stop it. When he came back to earth, he was tremendously strong. He knew how to split atoms with a thought. That alone was scary. When we saw what he did to Uziel, we understood what true terror was. Several of us ran and hid. Others stood their ground. We didn't stand a chance against that kind of power."

"He could split atoms with his mind? No fucking way!!! So he was like a walking atom bomb?" asked a rather impressed Sam.

"The atom bomb that humans made was based on plutonium. That was why it was so destructive. We didn't have plutonium six thousand years ago. But that didn't make his abilities any less lethal. By the time he finished, there were only seven of us still alive. We expected him to hunt us for our betrayal, but he didn't. Instead, the strangest thing happened. Ra just left. He flew off into the sky, and we haven't felt his presence since."

"That's a beautiful story Michael, but it still doesn't tell me why you can't die. It also tells me nothing about this other guy.... Ismael?"

Sam shoved the last bite of his burger into his mouth. He finally felt full. He sat back and adjusted his position to compensate for his now bloated waistline and let out a very deep and satisfying burp. Bringing his closed hand to his mouth to muffle the sound a bit, he noticed that the other diners were staring at him. They were all doing so in a way that made it look like they weren't staring at him. However, they were all terribly bad at the subterfuge and gave themselves away immediately. It only took Sam a moment to figure out what they were staring at.

At first, he thought it might be the empty plates that

filled the table from the multiple helpings of food he had just consumed. He knew it wasn't the incredibly good looking angel that was sitting across from him. Then it dawned on him. He was still wearing the blood soaked, sewer stained, rubble and dust covered clothes from the past two rampages he had been on. As he was glancing around the room at all the people staring at him, he caught sight of his reflection. Sam took note of the nappy matted blood soaked hair.

A change of clothes and a shower was definitely in order. Logically, it didn't make sense for him to go home and get clothes. By now they certainly knew who he was and would be looking for him at his house.

"Michael, I don't suppose you have a place that I could take a shower around here do you?" he asked

"Right. Walking around like this isn't quite appropriate, is it? Well, I don't live anywhere around here. I spend most of my time in luxury hotels." he remarked

"Luxury hotels? Are you some sort of millionaire?"

"No. I have absolutely no need for money. I pretty much just tell people what I want," Michael said.

"Really? Get the fuck out. You just tell people what you want, and they give it to you?" Sam paused for a moment and squinted his eyes in disbelief, "Bullshit."

"I told you I would never lie to you, Sam."

"Prove it," challenged Sam.

"Fine."

Michael raised his hand and gestured for the waitress. She rushed over to the table as if she were waiting on the president himself.

"What can I do for you?" she asked.

"Can you make sure that the manager takes care of our meal," Michael glanced over at Sam's face. He had a smirk that looked as if he were watching a cheap parlor trick. "and could you pour a cup of water on my friend here. Also while you are at it could you walk across the restaurant and pimp slap that smug looking bitch in the corner for me?"

"Sure. I'll be right back with that cup of water for your friend," she said.

As she walked away from the table, Sam cranked his head to watch the waitress walk across the restaurant to the table in the corner. Raring back her hand to last Tuesday, she slapped the unaware woman so hard it knocked her out of her seat. The form was so impeccable that the waitress looked as though she had been pimp slapping people for a living since she was two. The smack echoed off the walls and reverberated in Sam's ears. His eyes widened as he pulled his head back from what he saw. The waitress walked away back into the kitchen and disappeared for a moment.

Everyone in the restaurant was a gasp. Many of the diners simply couldn't believe that this random woman was slapped by the waitress. Several of them rushed over to console the woman now lying on the ground holding her face in pain. As they huddled around the woman, Michael began to take notice of the escalating situation he had just created.

"Well," he said, "this is about to get lively, isn't it?"

Michael stood up in the booth that he and Sam were sitting at. He took in a lung full of air and began to speak.

"Alright everyone, let's just calm down! Nothing you have seen is out of the ordinary. Everyone just go back to eating your food and forget about the woman that just got the bitch slapped right out of her."

It was like magic. Everyone stopped dead in their tracks and went right back to eating. There was a young man helping the slapped woman off the floor. He just let go and dropped her immediately. It was like Michael had some strange power of control over these people. Sam wondered what else he was capable of. He had already seen Michael's impressive strength, but this was something else altogether.

"How did you do that?" asked Sam.

"Quite simply. The power of suggestion. You've heard of that before right?" Michael said.

"Of course. I know what it is…. But I have never seen it work…" Sam leaned on the table "…especially not like that. How do you do it?"

"Through the power of my will. See most people, humans that is, have a relatively strong will power. But it only tends to get turned on when they are in a life or death situation. That will power can either be elevated or depressed over the period of a lifetime, depending on their particular circumstances." Michel took another pull from his beer. "Not only am I not human, but I have been alive a very long time. My willpower is on a whole other level. I can pretty much speak, and most people will do what I say."

"How come it doesn't work on me?" questioned Sam.

"Two reasons. First, Ismael forbade it. Second, technically your willpower is stronger than mine at this point, but since you haven't had much practice with it, I would say you have the will power of a twelve-year-old schoolgirl."

"What is Ismael's like? I bet he is way strong."

"Ismael can command matter into existence with a thought. As far as this planet is concerned, he IS the Lord, God. You and I are pointless specs of dust compared to him," scowled Michael.

Sam found this to be an intense response. He had never heard Michael be so deadly serious about something, even though he had just met him this morning. He was defensive about the subject of Ismael. Sam thought it best not to push too hard. Just then, the server came back over to the table.

"The manager said that this meal was on the house."

She then picked up Sam's water and proceeded to pour it all over his head. Michael giggled. The look on Sam's face was one of what the fuckery. He was obviously not happy about being soaked; however, he had been covered in so much stuff in the past twenty-four hours that it didn't matter. He pulled the napkin from his lap and used it to wipe the water from his face. He took in a deep breath and exhaled slowly to maintain his composure.

"So, tell me about why you can't die and who this Ismael guy is," said Sam.

"Ismael is the most powerful being I have ever encountered." Michael proclaimed. "He has ascended more times than Ra. If my guess is accurate, he has ascended ten times. I have no idea how he ascended the tenth time. Whatever killed him, it must have been powerful beyond comprehension. Currently, Ismael is the God of this world."

"This world?" questioned Sam.

"You don't think you monkeys are the only sentient beings in the universe do you?" answered Michael, "This planet has been visited countless times by any number of species. You guys are just too blind to see it."

"Hmmm, learn something new every day," said Sam.

"Anyway, about a hundred years after Ra disappeared; I was beckoned to the birth of a boy in the Middle East. I had no idea he was going to bond with the flower. Truthfully, I had no idea what the flower even was at that point. Ra was not very open about how he became what he was."

"For some reason, I could never get very far away from this young man. I watched him grow, day in and day out. He had two brothers named Cain and Able." explained Michael

"Wait. The Cain and Abel?"

"Yes, the Cain and the Able of biblical stories. They were Ismael's brothers. Ismael was the youngest with Cain being the oldest. One day they were traveling into a nearby town when a terrible storm struck. Though I tried my best to have very little interaction with the boy, I wasn't about to let him die in a sandstorm. So I helped them find refuge in a cave. It was in that cave that they found the flower. Neither Cain nor Able could pull it out of the ground, but Ismael had no problems pulling it out."

"As the eldest brother, Cain demanded that Ismael give it to him. When Ismael refused, Cain became violent. Able attempted to stop Cain from attacking Ismael but was killed in the process. Cain knew there would be consequences for killing Able and Ismael was the only witness. He struck Ismael over the head with a rock and left him for dead in the cave. What he didn't know was that the blood from Ismael's wound traveled down the cave floor and made a bond with the flower, much, in the same way, your blood did. When Ismael returned to the village the next day he said that he and his brothers had gotten caught in a storm and spoke nothing of the murders Cain had committed."

Michael continued, "Every day that passed, Ismael became smarter, stronger and more powerful. This not only made Cain insanely jealous but also drove him mad with paranoia. He fled into the desert in fear of Ismael revealing his secret and was not seen for several years."

"When he finally returned, both he and Ismael had grown into men. He asked Ismael why he never mentioned what happened in the cave. Ismael said that he had forgiven Cain, and there was no need to end his life over a mistake. That very same night Cain snuck into Ismael's room and cut off his head while he slept. It took almost a month for Ismael to ascend. He had to grow a new body. When he did resurrect, he was so disoriented he killed fifteen people in his village in a drunken power rage. He eventually caught up to Cain and attempted to kill him, but was unable to. Cain had spent the better part of a month cannibalizing Ismael's decapitated body. Something about that process had imbued him with immortality. Not only that but due to the sheer amount of Ismael's flesh that he consumed, he gained strength and wisdom as well. While he is not as strong as Ismael by any stretch of the imagination, Cain is still a powerful being, and each time Ismael becomes more powerful, so does Cain."

Sam sat motionless. He just had history re-written for him. It all made sense, but it was a lot to process. He opened his eyes wide and blinked a few times. This was turning out to be a hell of a day.

"Okay, I got all that. But you still haven't told me why you can't die," stated Sam.

"Because Ismael decided to keep me around." Michael evaded the question with all of the gallantries of a politician running for office.

"Come on Sam," said Michael as he stood up from the table. "Let's get you into something a little less obvious and a bit warmer."

"Warm? It's the middle of summer."

"Not where we are going."

Chapter 17: Burn the Others

A hot shower. Hands down, the most glorious thing he had experienced with his new found abilities. Every drop brought an exhilarating overload to his senses. From the temperature of the water, a perfect one hundred and six degrees, to the impact of it on the back of his neck. Everything about this shower was Heavenly.
To be able to feel the water drag the dirt and blood away from his skin was beyond refreshing. There were so many drops that he could hardly count half of them. His mind finally resolved to measure gallons per second instead of counting each and every drop.

Sam had never really taken a shower in a place this nice. His shit hole of an apartment was nothing compared to the five-star hotel that Michael got them into. As they walked in the front door, not a single person looked at Sam's blood covered attire. The front desk greeted Michael with a smile and gave him the penthouse suite for the price of asking. As they got off of the elevator, the hotel manager greeted them with a smile and personally escorted them to the front door.

The room was far more plush than a poor slob like Sam could have ever expected; truly the lap of luxury. White walls and white carpet. Durable and embellished couches and chairs populated the room instead of the cheaply made and poorly upholstered ones you might

find on the lower floors. Sam didn't even want to guess what this room cost per night.
Michael sent him to the shower straight away before he even got the chance to explore the rest of the massive room. The bathroom itself was divided into three rooms: one for shitting, one for showering, one for shaving. All three combined were larger than his entire apartment. There were plush bathrobes and more towels than he could use in a week and a tub that sat next to the shower. If there was a Heaven, this was it.

The steam from his hour long shower filled the oversized room and made it difficult to see the opposite side when he got out. Though the luxuriousness of the place was bliss, he still felt uncomfortable and out of place. He couldn't shake the feeling that the police were going to bust in at any moment and kick them out. Even worse he had become a bit paranoid with his heightened sense of awareness and felt that the military was going to kick in the door and try to off him.

Looking down at the floor, he saw his pile of putrid clothing. Just the sight of them sent him on a rollercoaster rerun of the day. He had woken up covered in blood, sliced open his hands, fought an angel, found out he died and was resurrected as a god, found out he killed well over 30 people the night before, killed some more people today, jumped across the street from the window of one building and through the window of another, and had gotten into a high-speed chase with a helicopter. The best part of it all was that he was still alive.

Action movies couldn't even compare to that.

"Schwarzenegger is a bitch." he thought to himself. Looking over his skin, he saw no scars. The gunshot to his leg was little more than a red dot. His hands were completely healed. It was as though they had never been cut. In fact, he had no marks on his body of any kind. The mild but ever so annoying case of acne that covered his shoulders was gone. The odd mole just below his navel that had the weird split hair growing from it disappeared, with it, any trace of body hair. He was bare as a baby's ass. He was pleased however that he still had facial hair. The perfect five o'clock shadow. Not even his now superior mind could make sense of how that happened.

Those were not the only changes he noticed. Sam was shredded. He was in relatively good shape yesterday. But, today he was a fine specimen of a man. All of his muscles were very well defined and a bit larger than normal. A perfect body looked like this. He was cool with that.

All of these new things were mere distractions from the real things he needed to think about. What was next? You can't do the things he had done in the past twenty-four hours and stay in the same place. Ascending God or not, there are always consequences for one's actions. Today his actions would no doubt bring severe consequences. He was going to have to leave. That was a no-brainer. Michael mentioned earlier that they were going somewhere cold. But where?

Sam had no qualms about leaving this city. He had always thought there were too many hipsters here anyway. The crime was bad, cops were dicks, rent was high, and the weather sucked. In fact, there was only one anchor he had here. Julia.

The events of the day had not quelled this young man's burning desire to be with her. If anything, his ascension made the love he had for her twice as strong. He now had the courage and confidence she was looking for. If he ever had even the slightest chance of winning her heart, it was now, assuming she was okay being with a mass murdering demi-god and his overly sarcastic angel sidekick.

Even if he managed to convince her that murdering dozens of people was not his original plan for the day, how would he keep her safe? Malice was now a thing that had to be dealt with, and he didn't want that monster anywhere near her. He also wasn't keen on the idea of having the military shooting at him with her around. What if she were shot?

That was enough to tell him what he needed to do. He needed to leave. Though it pained him to think about it, he was going to have to leave and never be around her again. At least, that is what a logical person would do. This was not what a man in love was going to do. He was resolved to leaving; however, a proper confession of his love was in order. She was worth the risk.

Sam stepped out of the bathroom into the massive space of the super plush hotel room. Laid out on the bed was a brand new outfit. A stylish pair of overly expensive but comfortable jeans, a T-shirt (that probably cost too much money), socks and a new pair of shoes. On them was a note written in the most perfect handwriting Sam had ever laid eyes on.

Burn the others. Order some food. I will be back in a few hours. -Michael-

Chapter 18: Containment

"Is it necessary for us to meet like this Michael? You know, I have a very nice office downstairs," said Cain.

"I don't have a lot of time," said Michael as he landed on the roof of the Cain building for the second time today.

"Funny, I thought time was your most abundant commodity. Why did you have me come up here? You could have just called. They have these marvelous little inventions called smart phones now. They are quite amazing."

Cain's sarcasm was thick. It reeked of contempt for Michael.

"I am here to discuss Sam."

"Wow. It has been what, about four hundred years? No time to catch up with an old friend? Always straight to business."

"Sam is far more powerful than Ismael was. I am going to need help containing him," said Michael.

"Containing him? I thought you were just in the record keeping business Michael. Did my dear brother change your job title?" Cain fired back.

"You know the plan as well as I do Cain. He doesn't have much time to prepare. Ismael has ascended again; that means this is a bit more serious than we thought."

Cain's jaw tensed for a moment. Though his brow was scowling, Michael had a point. Five thousand years had taught him many things. His extended life on this planet had made him a highly educated and wealthy man. It taught him a great deal of patience and understanding. He had become a shrewd, cunning and ruthless businessman.

He spent the past century building a massive empire. Cain was always learning and growing. However, the most important lesson he had learned in all of his time on this planet was that the word of God, his brother, was never wrong.

"The seed you planted germinated, but it took on its own life and personality," said Michael

"Interesting," Cain said as he stroked his beard. "That's the funny thing about seeds of the soul Michael, once you plant them, they need good conditions to grow in. Otherwise, they bear rotten fruit. Ismael knew what was going to happen even before that boy was born. If he wanted a different outcome, he should have done something about it. I simply did as I was told to do," explained Cain.

"That may be the case; however, if we don't contain Sam, he is going to destroy this planet before they do. I need your help to make sure that doesn't happen."

"Oh, come now. He can't be that strong yet. Surely, you and the Chinaman can babysit him for a few years. I have a lot to do. Global empires are rather time consuming." chided Cain. "I would, however, like it if you could kindly keep him away from my property."

Cain gestured to the door that Sam knocked off its hinges earlier that day.

"Sam is not in control of himself when he ascends. Malice, the seed, wields his power with lethal force." Michael said, "If we don't get him under control, you'll have a lot more than a little property damage to deal with."

"One funny thing about people Michael, if they get scared, they buy more guns. I am in the weapons business. Do you have any idea how much our stocks have gone up since last night? Monsters are good for business."

"Will you help or not?" Michael commanded an answer from Cain.

He knew it was a long shot asking Cain to help. However, Cain was a powerful being. He shared in the power of Ismael even though he was not given a gift; he stole it.

"What's in this for me? I have watched my brother shirk his responsibility to this planet for two thousand years- just because the Romans killed his Herald," Cain said with an angry tone.

His eyes lit up with a ferocious glow as he slowly advanced towards Michael with a dominance.

"I have spent the last thousand years cleaning up this planet through war, disease and famine. I even handled Lucifer when the rest of you couldn't. Then my dear brother shows up out of the blue and starts giving orders. I did what I was told to do. I am done taking orders from him. And I am certainly done listening to you. I will deal with Sam when he becomes a threat to me, or I find a use for him."

Michael and Cain exchanged glares at each other for a brief moment. There was something stirring inside of Cain that gave him the chills. Ismael's ascension caused Cain's power to grow tremendously. Michael could sense it. This conversation was not a good one to pursue. Cain was a far superior being to Michael, and the angel had obviously stepped outside of his boundaries. If Cain were going to help, it would be on his terms and in his way. There was nothing more Michael could do. He needed to get back to Sam.

"Cain, you are still alive because Ismael wills it. He has a purpose for you being here. You know the plan. We need you to help us save this planet. I hope that when the time comes, you will do what your Lord, God asks. I would hate to see you burn like Adriel."

Michael turned and flew away, frustrated with his encounter. He had hoped it would have ended better than it did; still, he expected much less. If Cain were not going to help, he would need backup from someone else. He only hoped that that someone else would make it in time. He had no idea when Malice would rear his ugly head again.

Chapter 19: I Love You

Michael put up some resistance to the idea of coming to see her. The humans had gotten clever at predicting each other's movements and habits. He knew they would find him here. The conflict was inevitable. Nonetheless, the decision was not his to make. Record and guide, that's all, nothing more.

There was not a quiver in Sam's body. His nerves were that of steel as he stood on the corner of the rooftop looking at her apartment from several blocks away. Even though the smog of the city hung thick in the midsummer air, Sam's vision was stronger than an eagle's eyes searching for prey. He could see the nondescript vans parked in various locations around her apartment. He knew with absolute certainty that there were swarms of heavily armed men inside those vehicles. This was going to pose a problem.

Sam closed his eyes and listened. The sultry air was jam packed with noise from the murmurs of the city. Squinting his brow and turning his head ever so slightly he could pick up the chatter from their radios, but could not make out their words. Though his ears were acutely sensitive, he did not have quite enough control to filter out the garbage.

He knew she should be there. Why else would they be hanging out near her place? That also meant that they knew who he was. But what Sam couldn't figure out was how they found Julia so quickly. Sam didn't own a cell phone. She wasn't on any record with him. He hadn't been there since all this began. How could they possibly know anything about his connection? They had an inside track. Someone was filtering them information.

Regardless, this was going to complicate the situation. Sam knew that his sudden disappearance would cause her to worry, and he wasn't going to have that. He had to say goodbye in person. It couldn't be a phone call or letter. Today could be the last time he saw her, and he had to tell her how he felt. She had to hear it from his lips.

He needed a solid plan. As he looked out and around, he began to see faint glimmers of light streaking out across the rooftops. They appeared and disappeared swiftly. A brisk squint of the eyes and shake of the head did nothing to cure this ailment. In fact, the harder he tried to focus on the task at hand of finding a way into his beloved's apartment, the more he saw of the lines. Curiously, the glimmers of light were in direct correlation with the various plans he was calculating.

A bit more focus and he could see faint glimpses of the actions he was plotting. The streaks of light would guide him to a major action. Then he was able to see all things and possibilities in that area simultaneously from a first person point of view. The whole ordeal was fantastically disorienting.

Sam shook his head and squinted his eyes once more as he turned and stepped away from the ledge. A couple of deep breaths would pass before he would reopen them. Turning back towards the ledge, he decided that instead of fighting it, he would let the wave of predictions flow over him. His new vision was obviously one of the unexpected benefits of his freshly acquired power.

His eyes began to dart left and right with the ferocity of a mathematician trying to read a large equation on a chalkboard for the first time. Lines were streaking out in front of him in a clustered spider web pattern. Images of rushed movements and hurried explosions of speed flooded his mind's eye in scattered detail. He would always lose sight of a streak as it bent around a corner or passed by a van that was holding soldiers. He was able to make the assumption that he could not see beyond the unknown. Which he had no idea what was waiting for him around those corners and no idea exactly how many men were inside any of those vans.

If only there were a way to know what was going on in those vans. Then he might know what to expect and be able to predict the outcome of those actions. Then it dawned on him. Sam picked up one of the chicken nugget sized stones that littered the rooftop and vigorously hurled it at the closest of the vans that were slightly over two hundred yards away. The stone smacked the side of the van with a massive pop.

To his surprise, his idea worked like a charm. The

instant the stone struck the van, it released a beautiful bouquets of colors that functioned as a combination of sonar and infrared combined. The muddy mixture of colors showed him a brilliant picture of what was going on in the van. Eight men, heavily armed.

"What do you think they intend to do with all of those big guns?" Michael asked as he walked up to the edge of the rooftop.

"Can you see what's in the van?" Sam questioned.

"I can see anything you see when you focus that hard. But I've got to say, neither Ra nor Ismael had those fancy tricks."

"You mean the thing I did with the rock?" questioned Sam.

"I mean none of it. The rock, the streaks, the predictive visions. It's quite fabulous," Michael stated. "What's your plan?"

"I haven't figured it out yet. Any suggestions?"

"Yes, I could just fly you over there. Maybe drop you off on the roof."

The sarcasm was thick. Sam was taken at the simplicity of the plan. He was trying so hard to use his new abilities and bigger brain to solve the problem that he had forgotten about his new winged companion.

"Sam, I would like to reiterate my previous statement about how bad of an idea I truly believe this to be," Michael's comment may as well have fallen on deaf ears.

Michael was not standing beside a rational man. Sam was a man that was driven by love. He had a fire in his heart for the girl of his dreams, and it was a fire that extinguished reason. Sam was a man that had a chip on his shoulder for authority and finally, he was a man that had something to prove and the power to prove it.

Michael was acutely aware of how this was going to turn out. He knew that you simply cannot give a child a big stick and expect him not to hit something with it. It was that way with Ra and Ismael. The question wasn't if he would hit anything, it was how many things would he hit before he stopped swinging.

Even with all these things taken into consideration, Michael wasn't there to talk him out of this love-stricken decision. This choice was as solid as concrete in Sam's mind. No, Michael's job was to observe and obey.

"Alright, let's do this," Sam said with a bit of a smirk.

Michael extended his arm, and Sam reciprocated with a forearm-to-forearm grip that would make the strongest Roman warrior proud. With a blast of air, they shot across the apartment littered cityscape below and hovered above the building in which Julia lived. A quick release and Sam came crashing down on the roof with a solid thud. He knew this roof and this building well. He was just a few strides away from the stairwell. His mind was filled with nervous tension at getting to see her. He had no doubt that he was going to tell her his true feelings. It didn't matter whether those feelings were reciprocated or not. He just knew that he owed it to himself to tell her.

Sam placed his hand on the door to the stairwell and a funny sensation washed over him. Something was not right. He could sense that going down those stairs was a bad idea. Maybe it was from the bad experience he had with the stairwell earlier. Perhaps it was more of the predictive abilities he just experienced a few moments ago. Whatever it was, the feeling was ominous and needed to be listened to.

Sam decided that a different way in was in order. Fortunately for him, Julia was not as poor as he was. She could afford to live in a building with balconies. He wasted no time. Running over to the edge of the building, he effortlessly climbed down three floors to his love's balcony. The whole thing reeked of Romeo and Juliet. The star struck lover scaling to his true loves balcony to bid her farewell. However, just like Romeo and Juliet, this was not a love story. It was a tragedy.

Landing on Julia's balcony, Sam knew that something was wrong. His new abilities and a quick tap of the window would reveal armed men in her apartment. Julia was on the couch. Her heart was racing with fear. Sam had no clue what they had told her. He wasn't so much worried about how he was going to save her; he was more concerned with the what they had told her about him. Had they made him out to be a monster? Were they telling her that he had killed people?

The suspense was killing him. He needed to talk to her. The smart thing to do would've been to leave and never return. Wash his hands clean of this girl and just be done with the whole thing. Then again, this was love. Sam had spent years building up his reputation, and he would be damned if he let some jarheads that didn't know a thing about him destroy the reputation he had spent so much time and effort building.

There was no thought put into how he was going to get in and save her. He only knew two things: Don't kill anyone and don't get shot. He breathed in a deep breath and went into action. Sam smashed the door off its hinges and sent it flying across the living room. The door slammed into two of the soldiers rendering them unconscious. Using wickedly fast speed, Sam darted into the living room and rendered one soldier unconscious with a swift shot to the face. The poor guy never saw it coming.

The next one was taken out with a shoulder throw that would leave him alive but deeply embedded in the hardwood floor of the apartment. The remaining two were eliminated with the flat screen TV and the DVD player being flung at ridiculous speeds across the room at them. All six men were immobilized, none of them were dead.

Taking a brief second to review the situation, he noticed that these were not the soldiers he had been fighting all day. These men were dressed differently and armed with what appeared to be more expensive gear. They were more like the men he killed in the stairwell at the Cain building. Further inspection of the unconscious soldiers would reveal the Cain logo on their shoulder patches. What were the Cain men doing here? Why would they be in Julia's apartment building? Something about this wasn't right. Were they working with the US military? Sam had lots of questions but now was not the time to answer them. He needed to get her out.

Julia was surprised by the chaos though it only lasted a couple of seconds. Just as she started to let out a colossal scream, Sam darted towards her and covered her mouth.

"Shhh," He placed his hand over her mouth. "I'm gonna get you out of here, but you gotta be quiet."

She was shaking in fear. Sam slowly removed his hand from her mouth.

"Sam!!! What are you doing here?" Julia said with a strong quiver in her voice. "You're not going to hurt me are you?"

"Hurt you? I am going to get you out of here. These guys have been shooting at me all day."

Sam didn't need anyone to spell it out for him. His fears were confirmed with her one pleading statement. They told Julia that he was evil and that he ruthlessly killed people. This fact was true; but, from Sam's perspective, this story was in serious need of some context.

"I am not what they say I am." he stated emphatically.

"But you killed all those people. They showed me the video! I didn't want to believe it, but then I saw your face and…"

Julia covered her face as the tears welled up in her eyes. Her heart was racing a million miles an hour causing her hands to shake in fear and disbelief.

"I will be happy to explain, but we've got to get the hell out of here before more of them come."

"Are you out of your mind?! Those men were here to protect me from you! I'm not going anywhere with you!" Julia said as she pushed him away. "Look what you did to them! I could barely even keep up with what you were doing. How can you move so fast?! When did you become so violent!?" she questioned him, desperately trying to make sense of it all.

"All this insanity started yesterday. It's a very wild story…but we don't have time right now." Sam said in a dismissive fashion as he reached for her hand.

"Was that you that killed all those policemen? You can throw cars?! They said you knocked a helicopter out of the sky!"

"Two actually," Sam retorted with a bit of a proud smirk on his face.

"What kind of trouble have you gotten into?" Julia questioned him further.

"Julia, I know they told you horrible things about me, but there is a lot more to it all than what they said," he hurriedly explained.

Sam was at a loss. He seriously believed that he was going to jump in here and tell her how much he loved her without any conflict. Instead, he had to break in, render six guards unconscious, just to have the love of his life shove him away. He needed to change her mind and fast.

Looking at her square in the eyes Sam implored, "I need you to calm down and listen to me."

Julia stopped thrashing and protesting. She became calm and sedate, never breaking her gaze from Sam's eyes. He was pulling a page from Michael's book of tricks. He was exerting his will over her. Coercion was not in the game plan. However, desperate times call for desperate measures.
"Sam, your eyes are so beautiful." she said in an almost hypnotic state.

"I am not the monster they make me out to be. You need to know that. I'm still me… I am going to get you out of here and then we can talk. The next few minutes are going to get crazy, so I need you to stay right behind me."

"Absolutely." she agreed.

Tuning his ears down the hall, Sam identified the familiar rustle of soldiers advancing towards the apartment. He needed a quick exit. With Julia in tow, he checked the balcony. He was strong enough to get both him and her down, but there was a large group of Cain soldiers amassing on the street below. Going out the hallway was not an option either. Sam's new found intelligence was quick to offer options.

Pushing Julia behind him for protection, he slammed his foot onto the floor repeatedly until a large hole opened into the apartment below. Sam scooped her up and dropped her through the new hole in the floor to the awaiting lower unit. Grabbing Julia by the hand and rushing to the door, he kicked it open, splintering the door frame in the process.

Exiting the doorway was like walking into a hornet's nest. There were already soldiers waiting in the hallway. Though he was caught off guard, he was able to dispatch them quickly leaving heads embedded in sheet rock and rifles broken across helmets. Each soldier was non-responsive, but still alive.

Julia was panicked. She had never been a part of this kind of ordeal. Though Sam was able to calm her down with suggestions, she was clumsy and scared. Sam was restricted to the limits of her movements as they dashed through the hallways. Every few feet he would have to stash or protect her. The numbers of Cain's men overwhelmed them in the narrow hallways. They seemed to be coming from every direction. From stairwells and apartment doors, hundreds of them poured into the building.

Each time they were cornered, Sam would blast another hole in the floor and escape to the level below. Each time they were met with hordes of Cain's men. Finally, they found themselves cornered on the ground floor.

There was only one way out. Sam was going to have to fight his way out through the front door. It seemed as though his day was stuck on repeat. Go into a building and get trapped by people trying to kill him. His brain went into overdrive as the first few shots whizzed past his head. He knew that he could heal pretty quick from a shot to the arm or leg, but he wasn't so sure about a shot to the head. And what about Julia? She was human. She didn't possess super strength, healing or immortality. He had to think fast to get her out of this trap.

They rammed through the door of the last apartment at the end of the hall. Scurrying to the far back bedroom, Sam placed her in the closet.

"I don't have time to explain. I didn't murder all those people like they say I did. Yeah, I killed them. But I want you to understand that it wasn't my fault. They killed me first," he explained to the frantic young girl.

"Sam, what are you talking about? How many people did you kill?"

"A lot. And it'll be a lot more if they kill me again. I just need you to stay here and hide."

Closing the door, he spun to confront the soldiers. Not one bit of fear ran through him. He had done his best to save their lives as he tried to escape, though it was looking like that option was now gone with the wind. He could hear them filtering into the apartment. The smell of their gun oil preceded them. He could hear the air being cut by their hands as they gestured signals to one another. The very presence of them made all of his senses tingle and dance. Nothing was going to stop this confrontation, and he knew it.

Sam's world went into slow motion again at the first sight of a gun barrel. This soldier wasted no words. Instead, he let his trigger finger do the talking for him. Several bullets exploded from the end of his gun.
There was no choice for Sam. He needed to stop them to save both himself and Julia. From deep inside, Malice's voice returned.

"I will show you power. Kill them and spit on their carcasses," Sam fought to keep the voice from distracting him from the task at hand though he couldn't hold back the surge of power building inside.

A brilliant burst of light exploded around him. The golden eyes that were focused with deadly intent morphed into a red glow. As the shots fired, he erupted into an impressive demonstration of speed. His hands were moving faster than the bullets that he swatted out of the air. More soldiers poured in, guns blazing.

Sam continued to track and stop the bullets that filled the space in front of him. Each and every bullet failed to hit its target. Except one. Though he was insanely fast, he watched in horror as one slipped past him. With every fiber of his being, he tried to catch that bullet. That one elusive bullet flew past him and pierced the closet door. There was no mistaking where it was going. The mathematical side of Sam's new brain calculated its trajectory down to a millionth of an inch.

Julia's head was directly in the path of that god forsaken bullet. Sam was helpless. He could not stop it. He could not catch it. He was about to lose the most important person that he had ever known, and he had to watch every agonizing moment in slow motion. To hear the bullet crack through the backside of the door was tormenting. Then he heard the most painful sound in all of existence. The bullet collided with her skull and splattered the other side of her head on the back wall of the closet.

There has never been a more gut-wrenching and furious

roar in the history of mankind. Sam's pain rattled the walls and floor, the plaster from the ceiling cracked and chipped, falling onto the heads of the soldiers.

The bullets Sam collected in his hands became projectiles that killed every soldier in the room with precision. His heart rejoiced in their deaths. A piece of him yearned to shred their dead bodies into a million pieces for what they had done. At this moment, Sam did not need Malice to fuel his anger. The contempt for their actions was enough to make him want to become a monster.

He turned and ripped the door of the closet off its hinges and flung it across the room.

Sam was without words. There she lay. Dead. He could not save her; he wasn't fast enough. Dropping to his knees in defeat, he pulled her close to his chest. Tears welled up in his eyes as his heart swelled with hatred and self-contempt. How could he have let this happen? Of all the bullets he caught, how could he miss the one bullet that mattered the most.

All he wanted to do was to tell this perfect creature that he truly loved her…that he loved her from the moment he saw her. To hold her in his arms and feel the kiss of her lips on his. Now he would never get that chance. The only thing he wanted to live for was gone.

"I love you," Sam said as he gently placed a kiss on the top of her head.

But this was not the place for him to stay and grieve. He did not have the time to stay and wade through this overwhelming grief that consumed him. He needed to escape and take her out of here.

He summoned his angel with the most somber of voices. "Michael."

He could hear more soldiers coming in the front door of the apartment. They were coming to finish the job. He knew Michael would make it in time, but there was a small sliver of him that just wanted to die. He knew that if he died, Malice would come and rip them to shreds. Malice would kill so that he didn't have to. It was a small shred, but it was there.

Michael burst through the window. He extended a hand to Sam.

"Come on, Sam. I'm so sorry about the girl. Let's get out of here," Michael's voice was comforting to Sam's ears.

He had seen everything that happened through Sam's eyes and he was well aware of the emotional stress Sam was enduring. There was no way to make the suffering stop. All the angel could do was offer a means of escape.

As if things could get no worse, they did. A single bullet was shot by a single soldier. And in a single instant, that bullet would change the course of human history. The bullet ripped through Sam's neck, shredding his carotid artery.

Chapter 20: Into the Furnaces

Sam had never known darkness like this. In all the violence and wrong doings that he had experienced in his short time on this planet, nothing had ever pulled the black veil over his heart like the one that covered it now. After what could only be considered the most valiant effort to protect the lives of those that sought to do him harm, he lost his struggle. The bullet to his neck caused him to bleed out faster than his body could repair the damage. As the last breath of air escaped from his lungs, he could hear the first beat of a darkened heart begin to pulse. There was no mistake. He did not need to guess what was going to happen next. He was about to die and go to Hell. No matter how hard he fought against it, the master of that Hell was about to be born again unto this world.

It was not a slow decent. As soon as his eyes shut, he was struggling against the tar-like viscosity of the black sludge. The last bit of light slipped from his eyes, and he wound up here, fighting and struggling for a single breath of air. Through his valiant efforts to escape this murky prison, he began to feel the hatred fill his thoughts. He started to curse his existence.

He was quick to blame God for putting him on this planet in the hands of such evil people. He cursed his broken mind for sending him to a place like this when he slept. He cursed the world that never understood what was happening, for never taking the time to see what was below the surface of a person that never wanted any of this.

His frustration was great. The powerful rush of self-loathing gave way to anger, and that anger gave way to strength. Sam burst through the surface of the black slop with a mighty thrust. His lungs expanded and pulled in a deep breath. He could feel the sting from the heat and ash that filled this world. The smell of sulfur penetrated his nose, almost causing him to vomit. His dilating eyes were filled with the sight of hundreds of screaming souls burning alive. Beyond those souls, all he could see was destruction. Crumbled buildings and great clouds of smoke filled the sky. Even with vision warped by heat distortion, he could see the enormity of the annihilation around him.

Each visit to the Furnaces was different. Most of the time the terrain was small and limited. However, in this visit, the landscape was vast and detailed. What Sam was seeing appeared to be the real world blended with his own private Hell. An overlay of what was happening on the outside. Was this the price the real world paid for his death? His inability to stay alive brought these consequences. All of these people died by his hand.

"Do you like what I have done with the place?"

Malice's words crackled across the sky like thunder. His voice sent shivers down Sam's spine. Pure evil has a sound to it that will make most men stop in their tracks, but Malice's voice made Sam want to put a gun in his mouth just to escape the boogie man.

Sam's personal demon was now in control of such immense amounts of power and from the visions Sam was seeing, it was using them to lay waste to everything around him.

A quiver took control of Sam's chin as he fought to keep the tears back. The wretched sound of Malice's words flooded his mind and heart with memories of abuse and torment at the hands of others. Horrid screams of both anger and pain perforated the air around him like howling phantoms come to steal his sanity. He was not safe, and this was not where he belonged. Summoning another burst of massive strength, he rocketed out of the black sludge with ferocious speed and crushed the charred ground beneath his feet as he landed.

The day's events had brought a new sense of confidence to him.
With another deep breath, he barked, "LET ME GO!!!!"

The sound of Sam's proclamation boomed into the void with a volume that almost rivaled Malice.

Before the echo could fade out, the ground began to tremble beneath his feet, giving way to a coffin-like box that pushed out of the ground and stood on its end facing him. Sam recognized it instantly. It was the box that he was locked in as a child. The smell of old rust and oil quickly permeated his nostrils, and the feeling of nausea and pure terror took the strength from his legs. Malice was attacking his senses to make him submissive.

Crouching slightly to keep from falling over, he gritted his teeth and curled his upper lip in defiance. The resolve that he wore like a mask said that he would not be taken down so easily this time. But what came next was more than he could handle.

The door of the box flew open with a thunderous crash and out of the abyss stepped a thing that was beyond terrifying. It had the shape of a man, covered in the same thick black sludge that Sam fought to escape from upon his entrance into this Hell. The sludge crept and slithered around him like a stream that fought to flow against itself. It was massive. The figure towered over Sam by several feet and looked down at him with disdain through a pair of wicked red, glowing eyes. A deep, guttural growl seeped through the sludge as the figure squatted sumo style in front of him. The two of them locked eyes through the waves of heat distortion and burning cinder. One with a look of pure intimidation and the other with a look of fear hidden behind a facade of resilience. Sam knew this thing could only be Malice.

Malice let loose a tremendous roar from a mouth that ripped open through the sludge that covered his face. Sam was pushed back, and as he held his stance, he left small trenches on the ground from his feet, which would not waiver.

Wiping the globs of blackness from his face, Sam did not break gaze from the monster that stood before him. Though he was scared as Hell, his sense of defiance was now in control. With a swift skip step that lead into a powerful lunging stance, Sam let loose a retaliatory roar. It was so loud that it pierced the air with waves of distortion and caused the sludge on Malice to ripple backward. This roar marked the first time that Sam had ever been able to make a stand against his captor. The first time that he showed his own power. The first time he ever resolved himself to fight, instead of run.

Malice did not budge.

Another low growl radiated from deep within the Hellish creature. A dead silence flowed through the Furnaces. Malice stood back up, towering high above Sam.

"Look at the brave little boy."

In a gesture of fear-fueled boldness, Sam raised his hand and extended his middle finger.

"FUCK YOU, YOU UGLY BASTARD!!!!" he yelled.

Sam took to the air once again with another powerful leap towards the head of the beast. Clinching his fist and thrusting it toward the towering creature's face, landing a massive blow. However, it failed. The effect that Sam was hoping for was not there. Instead of it wreaking havoc to his opponent, his fist, and the rest of his arm were swallowed by the black sludge. Unable to free himself, Malice whipped around and flung Sam into the box. The door slammed shut, and Sam was trapped once again.

The blackness that Sam had hated for so many years now completely engrossed him. There was no light. Just the muted rustling sound of his hands pressing against the inside of the box as he looked for a way out. The sound of the loose screws, nuts, bolts and razor blades that still littered the box filled his ears as they shifted around at his feet. The smell of rust and old oil filled the air once again, and eventually, so did the whimpers of a defeated little boy.

How long would he have to endure this misery? Was he meant to be in this box forever? Sam hammered his fists against the door of his wooden prison.

"Let me out!" he shouted. "You can't do this to me!"

His voice crackled with the sound of tears and submission. Even as a grown man, this box would reduce him to a fear-filled child. The strength and resilience he had for all of the evil things in his life did not aid him once the lid to that box shut.

His prison began to shift and move, dashing him against the sides as if it were being tossed around in the ocean.

The motion finally stopped as it barreled to the ground. In a sudden burst, one of Malice's massive fingers crashed through the door, nearly poking out one of Sam's eyes and filling his face with sludge and splinters. Retracting his finger, the sludge from Malice glistened around the hole that now allowed light to pour in. The soft amber light turned red as it was replaced by one of the monster's massive glowing eyes.
"I am not doing this. You are doing this to yourself, boy," growled Malice. "We are the same person. You created me to protect you from those that tortured you. You made me to punish those that hurt you. My anger is your anger."

Malice pulled his eye away from the hole in the door. Sam was quick to look out the hole because the darkness of the box frightened him so much. What he saw on the other side of the door was worse than a nightmare. It was a scene from his past. A jaded memory that fractured his soul and left a scar on his back.

Chapter 21: The Birth of Malice

> *"Prick your finger it is done...*
> *The moon has now eclipsed the sun...*
> *The angel has spread its wings...*
> *The time has come for bitter things."*
> *-Marilyn Manson-*

Sam stared out of the box, riddled with nervous tension. This place was hidden deep in his mind. Though he recognized it instantly, he avoided thinking about it whenever he could. Through the sludge ringed hole, he could see the kitchen of the house he grew up in. The smell of bacon grease always filled the air. It stained the walls in the tiny, unventilated torture chamber. This scene was all too familiar, one of the many verbal assaults that he endured in this horrid room.

This onslaught was particularly horrid. He had forgotten to do a particular chore. He couldn't even remember what the fuck it was he had forgotten to do.

"You worthless piece of shit. You make me sick! How could you forget to do something so easy? I feed you and clothe you, and all I ask you to do is some simple chores! But I guess you are too much of a fuck up like your father," his mother shouted at him from little more than a few inches in front of his face.

"Back off you BITCH!" Sam retaliated from inside of

the box as he hammered his fist into the wood that separated him from this memory.

He hated watching this and feeling so helpless, just like he did as a child.

"Come here you little pussy!" she barked as she locked her hand around a fist full of Sam's hair.

With a furious pull, she slammed the scared little boy face first into the wall, breaking his nose. Both Sams began to cry. One from pain, the other from anger. The one in the memory because of the impact. The one in the box because he knew what was next.

"You are such a little bitch! I never should have fucked your father. Then I wouldn't have to deal with your pathetic ass. I can't believe you are crying like a baby. I wish you would just die so I could get on with my life instead of having to take care of you. You want something to cry about?"

She grabbed a cast iron skillet that had been cooking ground beef for whatever the evenings meal was going to be and proceeded to violently beat Sam with it. The Sam trapped within the confines of the box could hear the "ding" of the frying pan as it collided with the various parts of his scrawny body. He watched as his younger self was beaten to the ground with swing after vicious swing of the pan.

Finally, when he was curled into a little ball, she mounted him. Placing one of her knees on his neck and the other on his back.

With the ruthlessness of a warlord, she drove the flat side of the pan down onto Sam's back. The heat from the pan seared and cooked his flesh. The boy in the memory screamed in blood-curdling agony. The one in the box, mortified, covered his nose and mouth to block the smell of burning flesh.

She ripped the pan off of his back, pulling with it pieces of charred flesh that stuck to the bottom. Backing away only a few steps, she threw the pan at Sam. The boy in the memory twitched and cried in pain. The man in the box became enraged. His mother looked dead square at the Sam inside of the box, and bum rushed it. Staring straight into the hole.

"You fucking pussy. You don't have the balls to raise a hand to me; you are a worthless fuck," she said as she lashed out at him.

With eyes full of rage and tears, Sam pounded on the inside of the box.

"I will fucking end you, you evil bitch! I FUCKING HATE YOU!!!" he shouted from a mouth that was foaming with fury.

His crazy bitch of a mother ran back over to the boy on the ground in the fetal position and pulled him off of the floor by his hair. Dragging him like an animal across the kitchen, she slammed him into the door of the box. The boy landed just below the hole where Sam could see his younger self aggressively being choked by this ferocious, vile woman.

The memory faded to a bright white light that flooded into the box and all but blinded Sam.

Slowly his eyes adjusted to the light, only to see that there was no definition to this memory. Only an infinite white space and another younger version of himself, sitting in a fetal position. Bloody and beaten, he was whimpering from the soul-crushing experience that took place in the kitchen. Sam had no memory of this though it felt oddly familiar.

"Why are you crying little boy?" asked a voice from the expanse.

"I hate them." the boy replied. "I hate them, and I want them to die."

"Then why don't you kill them?"

"I'm not strong enough." Sam whimpered.

"I am strong. I could kill them for you."

Sam raised his head to see who was talking to him. Before him was a young boy that looked oddly like him. This boy was not cowered on the floor. Instead, he stood proud and tall. His skin was much paler than Sam's, with a milky texture, that was somewhat translucent. Through it, Sam could not see bone and muscle. Instead, he saw what appeared to be some sort of black flame that was undulating beneath the surface. This pseudo copy's eyes were filled with the same black substance that pulsed below its skin. The Sam in the box knew him instantly. This was Malice: the evil of all evils, the most unclean.

"I can bring all of your misery to an end," he said, crouching down in front of Sam. "I can make them suffer as they have made you suffer."

"I don't know. The worse they hurt each other, the worse they hurt me." moaned Sam "I just want it to stop. I just want to die."

"Why die, when you can bring so much more pain to them alive? If they smite you on one cheek, we will smash them with the other. We can bring such glorious misery to them in life, and such pain to them in death," growled Malice.

His grin, stretching from ear to ear, showed his hideous black mouth with jagged, sharp teeth protruding from his gums.

"We can do that?" asked Sam.

Malice giggled, "All that and so much more. You are destined for great things, Sam."

The young boy's eyes welled up with tears. Malice's words were the first compliment that anyone had ever given him. No one in his entire life had paid this much

attention to him. Here was someone that wanted to help him. Someone that saw his pain. The only person that ever recognized his real anguish. The overflow of emotion was strong enough to choke him up. All he had ever wanted his whole life was for someone to listen. Just to be wanted... to be heard.
But, the Sam inside the box knew this was a trick. Though this was a memory that he had never known, he knew the thing tempting him as a boy was a beast like no other.

"I want them to suffer... I want them to hurt the way they hurt me." the younger Sam sobbed.

With an angry spit filled scream, he shouted, "I WANT THEM TO DIE!!!!"

"Then let me help you. Let me hurt them for you. Just say yes." Malice said rising back to his feet. "Just let me in and I will do this for you."

"Is it going to hurt?"

"Only a little...just for a moment. Then you will feel much better, I promise."

A brief second of hesitation passed through the younger Sam. He knew what he wanted. Truthfully, he didn't care how he got it. He had been broken and beaten and saw no way out. The beasts temptation was the only option that he had ever been given. He may never get another chance.

"Yes."

The word was barely audible to the Sam in the box. However, he already knew the answer. And he was powerless to stop it.

Malice was quick to act. He jumped on top of the youthful Sam before the breath from speaking had finished escaping his lungs. Throwing Sam to the ground, he began to thrash and shred him in a bloodthirsty rage. Ripping massive chunks of flesh from the young boy's body and swallowing them whole. At first, the boy fought, but, seconds later there was no more fight.

The floor of the infinite white space was covered with splatters and pools of blood. This vicious monster continued to eat the young Sam until there was nothing left but bones and chunks of guts.

The Sam in the box could only watch with disdain.

Malice stood up once again, drenched in so much of Sam's blood that it dripped from his chin and fingers. Cranking his head at an inhuman angle, he looked directly at the box that Sam had been confined to.

"You are just a shadow of me." Malice hissed.

The infinite white space went dark as the floor opened into a whirlpool that sucked Sam's box down into it. On the way down Malice's voice pierced the sky once again.

"He is coming, and you can't stop him."

Furious and fed up with this uncontrollable trip through the dark recesses of his mind, Sam mustered up every bit of strength and focus he had. With one final burst, he crashed through the door of the box that Malice had trapped him in. However, his escape was not what he had planned. He came crashing out of the box into his childhood bedroom.

Erupting from the closet in a tangled mess of second-hand clothes, Sam stumbled into the small dingy room. The scent of mold and humidity, mixed with alcoholic sweat and cigarette smoke flushed into his nostrils. The poorly wallpapered walls were devoid of any decoration after various drunken rampages by his father had left any pieces of art or posters shredded on the floor. Only the little corners were left stuck behind the tape that Sam was too defeated to remove. The carpet was crunchy underfoot from various pools of vomit, blood, and spit that were barely cleaned after many nights of assault.

This place that brought back memories of terror along with the unshakable sense of impending doom. At any moment, Sam knew that a tornado of vile words and senseless abuse would come crashing through the doorframe that had no door.
Even now, after so many years, the older Sam was

nervous.

In the bed lay a younger Sam; black-eyed and still swollen a bit. Malice brought Sam to a time several years after the abuse in the kitchen. Half covered in an old blanket, laying on a pillow that was as crusty as the carpet. The pillow had the pleasure of having tears thrown into the mixture as well as the other bodily fluids on the carpet.

Sam stood at the end of the bed looking down at himself, not knowing why Malice chose to show him this.

The young Sam, still asleep, sat straight up in the bed. No yawns or scratching. No stretching or moaning. He stood up straight away and walked out of the room. The older Sam beckoned to him.

"Where are you going?"

He received no response. The younger Sam was sleepwalking, yet, he was sleepwalking with intent. As Sam followed the younger version of himself down the hall and into his parents' room, he became more and more worried. What was Malice showing him? What was the point of bringing him back here? Seconds later, he would get his answer.

Both Sam's entered his parents' room. One asleep and the other fearful of what he was watching. The younger Sam grabbed the half-empty bottle of cheap booze off the nightstand. He proceeded to jump up onto the bed and smashed it across his still sleeping father's head, leaving both his father and mother drenched in alcohol.

His mother woke up for a brief moment before Sam kicked her squarely in the jaw, sending her right back to sleep. He thoroughly tied the covers down across the two unconscious bodies lying in the bed. The older Sam knew what was going on, but remained motionless in the corner and not attempting to stop his former self.

Sam was witnessing a moment of reckoning. Judgment day for the filthy pieces of shit being strapped to the bed by the dog they beat. He had always wondered what happened, and now he was getting a front row seat to the show. His conscious self could have never mustered the courage to do something like this. It had to be Malice that was driving. Though he hated seeing what Malice did to the boy in the infinite white room, at least, he was delivering on his promise.

Once again, the young Sam jumped up onto the bed. He whipped out his penis and began to piss on their faces. It only took a second to bring them back into consciousness. Only a second more and they would realize they were not able to get out of that bed.

Sam reached into the pocket of his sweatpants and produced a Zippo lighter. He turned his head towards the older version of himself.

"This is why I exist. I am here to protect you. To make

you strong. To make you able to do the things you don't have the balls to do."

Again, the older Sam did not move. He simply watched. Everything he was watching had happened already. It was a set of events that had to play out. Even if he wanted to, he could not stop it. He would not.

The younger version looked back down at the heathens in the bed as they writhed and cursed like rabid dogs foaming at the mouth. The lighter that Sam held in his hand made a distinct sound as he flicked it open with his thumb. It made an, even more, distinct sound as he spun the flint to ignite the flame.

"I hope you like the feeling of being burned, bitch." the older Sam said in a cool and calm fashion.

When the younger Sam dropped the lighter, the flames did not start big like in the movies. Nevertheless, they grew fast. His parents' angry slurs turned to gut-wrenching screams of horror, then to the agonizing screams of being burned alive. The flames engulfing the room produced tremendous amounts of heat. The heat itself was not enough to make either version of Sam want to leave. Each of them had a cold, emotionless look on their face while watching the two revolting human beings burn to a crisp.

The younger Sam got right into the face of his older self.

"I get stronger each time you do, boy. I am not afraid to

use that power to protect us. They want to hurt us. I will make them pay."

Fade to black.

Chapter 22: The Second Petal

Michael stood over Sam and Julia's bodies. As Sam lay on the floor dying from the gunshot wound to the neck, his eyes glazed over with a dark tar-like substance. The blackness circulated like ink in water. Never still, always flowing. Though the flower was bringing him back to life, this was not Sam awakening, but Malice. He rose to his feet like a scene from a *Dracula* movie, ridged and stiff. The dust of crushed sheetrock and concrete left a cloud of smoke that undulated through the air behind his half-cocked head. A dark black and purple glow engulfed his body and whipped around like a gasoline fire.

Michael was scared. He knew this was not Sam, and he hadn't felt fear like this since Ra. The power that Malice was wielding at this point was tremendous. It began to radiate from him in a flaming black brilliance. Malice was not good, and this was almost palpable. The amount of will that he possessed at this point was enough to invoke nausea and vomiting on everyone within fifty feet of him. The soldier that shot him in the neck was no exception. He quickly dropped to his knees and yacked his guts out. Malice held out his hand, and the soldier lifted off the ground and shot across the room. His neck landed directly in Malice's palm. Effortlessly, he squeezed until the soldier's head, and body fell lifeless to the floor separated from one another.

"Calm down, Sam." Michael barked.

"Sam is hiding in his box," growled Malice. "I respect your power Michael, but if you don't leave I am going to kill you."

"You can't kill me, Malice."

The monster cranked his head over to look at Michael. He glared at him for a brief moment and wasted no words. With a simple wave of his hand, he sent the angel rocketing out of the building, breaking down every wall in his path. Michael was outmatched, and outclassed. Malice ascended to a far more powerful state than Ismael or Ra were at this point. The sheer amount of hatred that circulated through his veins was a driving force in his strength, and that strength was multiplied by the resurrection. There was no one else with any kind of power that was able to step in and stop him now. Michael did not have what it took. He was just going to have to let the monster have his way.

Malice giggled cynically for a moment. He was ready to unleash Hell, and he had the power to do it. With a deep breath and a powerful squat, he launched himself up through the many floors above him and rocketed out of the top of the building. At the apex of his jump, Malice surveyed the city below him. He saw how full of ignorantly blind people it was. Walking around like sheep without a shepherd. Silently judging one another with deceitful contempt. Oh, how he longed to slaughter them. To destroy those that had created him. Such a waste of air they were.

They needed to pay for their existence and Malice was about to collect on that payment. As he raced back toward the rooftop, he raised his hands above his head, both fists clutched. Upon contact with the roof, he smashed them down with a deafening impact. A thunderous crack followed. A boom erupted from inside the building as its very foundation exploded out from underneath it. The shrapnel from the explosion shredded the flesh of dozens of people at street level, breaking bone and tearing bodies in half with lethal and brutal force.

The building creaked, groaned and popped as it came crumbling down. Dust filled the air for blocks. Screams were heard from inside and outside the surrounding buildings. Beyond the screams and car alarms, there was an eerie silence. Malice stood atop the mound of steel and stone with a sickening, shit-eating grin. To Malice this was barely even a warm up. The hundreds of dead and mutilated bodies in the rubble were nothing compared to what he intended to do. He needed to slaughter them all. Everyone needed to die.

He picked up a truck-sized piece of concrete from the rubble of the building and hurled it like a Frisbee toward the building across the crumbled and broken street. This inhuman task was effortless. The impact caused a large portion of the building to collapse. Malice wasted no time. He could see the people inside their homes, scared and running for their lives. He waited for them to come flowing out the front door in panicked masses. As they did, he raced into the center of the crowd knocking those in his way down like bowling pins made of sand.

The blood from their eviscerated bodies covered the mass of panicked people and only caused the screaming to intensify. Those closest to the center tried to run, but it was pointless.

Malice began grabbing them and ripping them apart. In a dizzying flurry of body parts and blood, he shredded through dozens of people without a second thought. As they began to run, Malice raised his hand and beckoned them back to him. They would simply be pulled off their feet and fly backward into his grip, like a human yo-yo. It was in Malice's hands they would die, before they even knew what had happened. No one who came out of that door survived.

Malice stood in the center of the shredded pile of dead and dying people saturated in blood. Some were writhing in agony, others twitching as the nervous systems sent the last impulse of electricity. He breathed in a deep breath through his nose with a sense of pleasure; much the same way someone enjoys the bouquet of a great wine. He reveled in the smell of blood. But this would not be the end. There was still so much more to do. This place needed to look like the Hell he was from. There was no ash or cinder in the air. The smell of burning flesh and sulfur did not singe his nose hairs. He needed to change that.

Hell needs fire, and now that he was all warmed up, he was going to give this place the makeover it needed. Stepping over broken and dismembered carcasses in his way, Malice casually walked out into the middle of what used to be a street. A single swish of his hand would push away all the dust in the air and send all of the debris and busted cars tumbling away from him. With another gesture, the asphalt cracked and floated up and away from the ground leaving only dirt and broken gas lines spewing massive amounts of the noxious fumes into the air.

With but a thought, Malice created a flame from thin air and ignited the gas. The explosion was horrendous. It shattered windows for blocks and scorched the surface of every building that was in sight. Malice needed this. Carnage and chaos. Misery and agony. His need to spill blood could not be satiated.
He knew that men would come to destroy him. They would bring their guns to try to kill what they did not understand.

If he listened close enough, he could hear the sound of tanks and armored vehicles making their way to combat what the media would later declare an unknown source of pure evil. A slight smirk gave but a glimpse into the excitement that was building inside of this monster. They would flock to him like lambs to the slaughter, and he would paint the streets red with their blood. The sounds of sirens and helicopters filled the air. First responders were gallantly racing to the scene to save lives and protect their beloved city. They were unaware of what they were charging into.

When the first set of police, firemen and paramedics showed up, they were overwhelmed by the carnage. It was difficult to know where to begin. There were so many dead that there was hardly anyone to save. The horror of the situation was nauseating. Malice waited for them to draw deep into his trap. The glow that surrounded him went away. He simply went dormant to lure more people closer. He struggled to contain his power and rage until just the right moment. Motionless, he waited for their approach.

A pair of firemen were the first in the vicinity. Assuming from the amount of blood that was on him, they needed to check if he was alright. To them, he looked like a victim. Half burned and caked with blood and dust; they barraged him with questions. He did not answer. He did not move. They attempted to move him, though, it would be the last mistake they would ever make.
Malice grabbed them both by the back of the head and collapsed their skulls together and threw their bodies away like useless ragdolls.

Several policemen saw the two firefighters die and drew their weapons immediately. They began shouting at him to get on the ground. Another police officer turned and recognized him as the monster from the previous evening's slaughter.

"That's him!!!" he shouted, "Shoot that bastard!!!"

The small group of policemen quickly turned into a larger group, and they all began to fire at Malice. Each officer unloaded their entire clip on him. Not a single shot made it through. Each and every bullet stopped midair around fifteen feet in front of him. Malice remained motionless. They had all advanced close enough to him. He was ready to spring his trap.
The purple and black glow burst outward and began to undulate around him once again. The men and women closest to him instantly became nauseous, dropping to their knees, vomiting uncontrollably. Malice wasted no time. He darted towards the closest officer and punted him into a building over three hundred feet away. The next officer was able to fight through nausea and reload his firearm. He was also able to squeeze off six shots before the monster made his way to him.

Malice was un-phased by the gunfire and squatted down in front of the kneeling officer.

"Kill yourself." Malice whispered to the officer with a deep growl.

Without any hesitation, the officer pulled the gun up to his head and pulled the trigger.

Killing each of these men one at a time was a bit too time consuming for his liking. He needed more destruction, more death, and more conflict. Waving his arms again, he sent every one of the remaining officers tumbling hundreds of feet away with tremendous force.

The sounds of armored vehicles drew ever closer. He could feel the fear of the soldiers and the glee of their commanders that were about to get the opportunity for combat. Malice became elated. He saw an opportunity to stretch his wings and put this amazing power to the test. He wanted a chance to show off how strong he had become. In his eyes, he was a God, and his wrath was mighty. He would instill fear in every last person. If he were going to turn this place into Hell, he would need a lot more destruction and death than this.

Chapter 23: Fucking Hostile

On tracks of steel and thick treads of rubber came the forces of man. With guns heavy in hand and high caliber, fully automatic firepower mounted to the top of armored vehicles, they advanced. Hundreds of soldiers came to face the threat that was Malice. The military had never faced an adversary like this. This was a new experience for every one of the soldiers.

Today they were not fighting another army. There was no terrorist plot. They were not up against a militia. Before them was one man. One that glowed in a dark purple flame.

Victor tried his best to remain calm. He pulled a handkerchief from the inside of his body armor. His hand was shaking from fear and a bit of shock at what he was seeing. Raising his trembling hand to his forehead, he wiped away the sweat and dust from the crumbled building that he narrowly escaped. This moment would shape the rest of his life, however, short it may be.

Victor stepped out in front of the advancing force, dropped his rifle to his side and raised a fist to those behind him as a signal to stop. In a calm, non-aggressive fashion, he approached Malice. For some reason, the monster had spared his life before. It even attempted to communicate with him by putting thoughts into his head. If there was even a chance to stop him through reason, he had to try.

Malice allowed Victor to approach, yet raised his chest defiantly as he got about twenty feet away. Victor's heart was racing out of control. The silence was deafening, broken only by the sounds of flames whipping and tiny pieces of rubble crackling under his feet as he adjusted his weight. His choice may very well have been the most foolish thing he had ever done. What do you say to something that brutally slaughtered so many people?

"Will you stop?" he asked.

"Why should I?" said Malice. "Your people continually try to kill me, even when they know they can't."

"It's because you scare the shit out of us. My commanding officers see you as a threat. Their job in life is to kill threats. But if you calm down, maybe we can stop this before it gets real ugly." pleaded Victor.

"There is only one solution. I am going to tear every single one of you disgusting insects limb from limb. There is no calm. There is only Malice."

Victor realized that negotiating with this monster was pointless when Malice raised his hand and flung him backward over a hundred feet. Crashing into the group of soldiers like a bowling ball was the only thing that saved him from breaking limbs. Taking a moment to gather himself, Victor stood up and breathed a sigh of frustration. This asshole has killed way too many motherfuckers to be still breathing; he thought to himself. Time to bring down the hammer.

Looking back over his shoulder at another soldier behind a very large gun, he said, "Light that fifty up. I've had enough of this motherfucker today."

As the massive fifty caliber rapidly blasted bullets at Malice, a smirk of superiority grew on the face of Victor. The stout rounds of ammunition easily made contact with the monster, sending him sliding back. Within the first few shots, Malice was on his knees.

Nudging the soldier next to him, Victor joked, "He didn't want any of that, Ma Deuce," Referring to the powerful M2 .50 caliber gun.

Several soldiers nervously laughed. Their laughter would be short lived. Malice stood up, much to the surprise of the soldiers.

Slamming both of his fists into the ground, he caused dozens of small stones to jump off the ground. With a short and vulgar shout, the stones became projectiles that shot towards the soldiers with Malice trailing right behind them. Heads and limbs were rendered from bodies on impact from the stones. Malice rushed the large gun that shot him, grabbed it by the barrel, ripped it from the vehicle and began to smash soldiers at random with the hunk of machinery. The armored vehicle tried to leave, and Malice smashed it as well.

Victor fell to his back in the fray. While Malice was distracted by the vehicle, he was able to launch a grenade from his gun into the belly of the rampaging beast. The explosion sent the monster tumbling. No seconds were wasted; soldiers opened fire on him with everything they had. The mass of smoke was thick and hid Malice's next move. Out of the smoke came several car-sized slabs of asphalt that decimated the soldiers by the dozens.

This type of violence was what Malice was built for. He loved every second of it. The feeling of making his enemies suffer by his hands resided at the very core of his being. He knew no mercy. He possessed no sympathy. He belched out a massive howl of elation. Playtime was just getting started. There were countless more to kill and though he was enjoying slaughtering these few by hand, it just wasn't gratifying enough. There needed to be more dead, faster.

Flexing his muscles, the back and purple flame of energy that radiated from him burst into a bright green. Malice charged into the wall of the building beside him, leaving only dust and rubble in his path. Once inside, he forcefully smashed into every wall and support beam. This building was coming down and so was everyone in it and around it. Only seconds after blasting into one side of the building, he erupted from the other side, tackling the parked cars and soldiers in his path.

The rumble of the building was startling to anyone that heard it. Victor shouted to all of the men around him to run. Only a few were able to escape the collapse.

The twelve story building came down with a thunderous boom, sending massive clouds of billowing dust out like waves through the streets and alleys for hundreds of yards. The screams of the hundreds of people trapped inside were never heard, and the ones from around the base of the building were quickly muted.

The Military never stood a chance. Mankind didn't possess the weaponry nor the intelligence to handle such a hostile force in such close quarters. They were useless.

From afar, Michael watched as Malice continued to kill people mercilessly and at random inside of the smoke. Though they could not see nor hear the monster coming due to the zero visibility of the smoke, the rampaging demon could see them quite well. Michael's job was to record, but he was in no mood to recount this horror. He knew he was no physical match for Malice. He did, however, have an ace up his sleeve in the form of backup, he only needed to buy time until it arrived. Michael was going to need to slow Malice down, in the same way, he had done earlier.

Michael was going to need to be swift and clever about his timing. He had no doubt in his mind that this was going to be a difficult proposition. He needed to try. He never had a problem watching humans die, especially if it was due to their own stupidity. He also never interfered where there was an opportunity for humans to help themselves. However, this was a situation that demanded action from him.

Michael spread his wings in a powerful fashion that was befitting of an angel. Leaping from the rooftop where he had been observing the chaos, he rocketed down to the scene, landing inches behind Malice.
Malice instantly spun to face Michael. The angel immediately slammed the palm of his hand onto Malice's forehead. He was going to try and put this beast to sleep as he had done before. But, this time, he would have no luck.

Malice batted Michael's hand away with defiance. The force of the blow ripped the angel's arm off just above the elbow. His eyes grew wide with utter disbelief. Nothing on this planet had ever done this much damage to him, and with a single blow no less. He knew Malice was powerful, but this was on a whole other level. Malice's attack didn't stop there. Michael could see the next punch coming straight for his face. Its speed was remarkable.

The angel would barely have time to move his head to the side before the glowing green fist shot past. The force of the missed blow was enough to rip the flesh from Michael's neck, shoulder and jaw while sending him hurling down the street. He erupted out of the billowing smoke just before beginning an uncontrolled tumble for several more blocks. Michael had tried and failed to slow the beast. For a moment, he felt hopeless.

What on this planet could stop this monster from continuing his rampage?

Then he remembered. He had backup.

Chapter 24: The Master and the Monster

A streak of brilliant white light shot from the sky with a crack of thunder in tow. It landed several feet from Malice, fracturing the concrete and sending out a shockwave that would clear the air for hundreds of yards.

Inside of the brilliant white light stood a man that appeared to be in his thirties. His hair was jet black though the glow from the light made it difficult to tell. His mid-sized stature draped in loose clothing that flowed in rhythm with the surrounding light. As it moved over the surface of his body, it would reveal chiseled muscle tone underneath. His posture was one that displayed authority and control. It wreaked of technique and intent.

This was the backup Michael had been waiting on. This force was going to bring control to this situation. This was a true master of combat.

This was Wei Jin.

"I told you all that power was nothing without control. Now look at the mess you've made," said Wei Jin as he reduced his glow and waved his hand dismissively at Malice.

"It is going to take these people years to clean up and

rebuild after this."

Wei Jin's confidence seemed to infuriate Malice. He lunged at the master with a flurry of blows. With one hand behind his back, the master of combat blocked and deflected each one of them with little effort, lecturing the monster in the process.

"Good. I see power, speed, emotional intent, but you lack a few things," he scolded. "You have no control. You attack like a ravenous dog. Unskilled."

Wei Jin blocked several more of Malice's blows before retaliating with one of his own. An open palm strike to the beast's torso sent him spinning away through the walls of yet another building. He followed the spinning mass of monster into the building. This opponent was easy to control but needed management to minimize any further damage.

Malice landed on his feet ready to fight. Pulling the stone from the walls, he hurled them at Wei Jin. The masterful fighter did little to dodge them. Evading most of them by millimeters and crushing the rest with one hand still behind his back.

"I see you have discovered shifting; without a teacher no less. Impressive. But, you still lack control, as well as creativity. Allow me to give you a lesson." he said, casually wiping the dust from his shirt.

Malice lunged at Wei Jin with the intent of ripping his

head off. However, he countered with the simplest of throws, sending Malice tumbling back out into the street. The toss would hardly slow the monster down. Malice stomped the ground and caused a large piece of asphalt to rise. Sinking his hands into the soft stone he spun and hurled it towards the opponent.

Wei Jin stopped the stone midair with but a wave of his hand. Closing his fist, he caused the boulder to split into hundreds of tiny pieces and with another flick of the wrist they dropped to the ground. Wei Jin sped into Malice's personal space and gripped him by the throat, delivering a series of earth shattering blows. The hits made short work of the monster and knocked him unconscious. Wei Jin set him down graciously.

Seeing that the monster had been put to sleep, Michael flew into the scene.

"Are you alright Michael?"

"I am fine. My arm will grow back soon enough," Michael said gesturing to his severed arm and damaged neck.

"Thank you for showing up. He is vastly stronger than I imagined."

"That's because there are two of them in there. This one can pull power from the other, thus multiplying his power exponentially," said Wei Jin. "If he were properly trained, he could keep up with Ismael at his sixth ascension."

"You think he is that strong?" questioned the angel.

"He can solid shift naturally, from pure emotion. The boulders he was throwing were quite heavy, which means he has a rudimentary use of gravity shifting as well. He will far surpass the power of our Lord," Wei Jin knelt down beside the unconscious Sam. "However, this monster that resides in his mind has taken on a life of its own. The two will need to learn to coexist, or his anger will destroy the entire world."

"Fantastic. Now I have to keep up with both of them." Michael stated with a heavy dose of sarcasm.

"I thought your job was to record."

"Last minute change of plans. It is now my job to be a guide as well. Ismael wants me to keep a close eye on his development. He wants to watch through my eyes," explained Michael

"Better through your eyes than in person. These people are not prepared to witness the Lord again, especially since his latest ascension," warned Wei Jin.

"Speaking of the latest Ascension, I like the new glow. It was rather impressive to see you in action."

"It is a byproduct of his gift to us. I am sure you felt it as well."

"Yes, but I didn't acquire strength or a fancy glow like you. Mine is something...different," Michael said in a concealing tone.

He too had grown in power with Ismael's most recent ascension, though he wasn't quite ready to showcase his newly acquired skill set.

Wei Jin scooped Sam up under the arm, lifting him with little effort.

"We need to take him to my temple. He must be trained before he unleashes destruction on this world again."

Suddenly a voice boomed from behind the smoke, "You are not taking him anywhere just yet."

Michael and Wei Jin snapped their heads to see a well-dressed figure walk out of the smoke. Both of their hearts dropped when they realized who it was.

"Ahhh fuck," exclaimed Michael.

Wei Jin was a bit more formal in his greeting, "Cain. It is good to see you. I believe the last time we met was in 1556."

"China, that was a hell of a fight. Took me almost a year to regrow my foot. How many died in that earthquake?" asked Cain

"Almost a million." Wei Jin solemnly stated.

"Funny thing about these ants. Kill a bunch of them and they just multiply faster. I tried to warn Lucifer about that whole plague thing, but he just wouldn't listen. Now we are dealing with over seven billion of these sacks of shit."

"What do you want, Cain?" questioned Michael accusingly.

"I just need to borrow Sam for a few moments," Cain raised his hands, sending Wei Jin and Michael flying backward. The force of Cain's power pinned them to a wall.

"Don't worry, I will be done in just a second."

"What are you doing Cain?" shouted Michael

"You asked me for help containing this monster. You want containment; this is what it looks like."

Cain grabbed Sam's unconscious body off of the ground by his throat. Sam could offer no resistance. The powerful blows from Wei Jin's fists left him helpless. Cain placed his hand on top of Sam's head and twisted until his decapitated body fell to the ground.

Michael shouted "NO!!!"

Cain released his grip on the angel and the Wei Jin. He

casually tossed the head of Sam at their feet.

"If memory serves me right, you've got about a month before he wakes up. That should be plenty of time to get him away from the masses and teach him how to control that ridiculously clumsy beast of his." Cain said while reaching over to grab Sam's headless body. "As for me, I have just gotten myself a light snack."

Michael lunged at Cain, only to become paralyzed midair.

"Come now, Michael. I already have one angel on my mantel. There is always room for another."

Michael fought hard against the paralysis. He twitched and groaned as he tried to muscle his way out of it. Cain slung Sam's body over one shoulder as he walked across the rubble bringing himself face to face with the suspended angel.

"Stick to the plan, Michael." Cain scolded "If you are lucky, this guy will give you a gift, too."

With a sudden burst of air, Cain shot off into the sky and quickly vanished from sight. Michael fell to the ground. He laid there for a moment.

"Well, that didn't go so well." he said with his face in the dirt.

Wei Jin walked over to Sam's head and picked it up off

of the ground, "This boy is going to need a herald. He will be too strong to address his people when he wakes up."

Michael lifted himself off the ground with his one remaining arm. "I have just the guy for the job," he said as he stumbled to his feet.

"We should take him with us. He'll need to make the bond before Sam wakes," said Wei Jin.

Michael flew to the spot where Malice had encountered the first group of soldiers. Lying there, beaten and bloody was Victor. His eyes grew wide with fear as the angel landed in front of him. He scooted and scurried as he attempted to load his gun, grunting in disbelief of what he thought was certain death.

"Victor Ruiz. Your Lord God has a need for your services," said Michael with all the glory befitting an angel.

With his one remaining hand, he grabbed Victor by his body armor. Thrusting his wings with a single powerful beat, they soared off into the sky.

12 Blackened Petals

The Gospel of Sam: Book Two

Book Two: Hell Behind the Blackness

Sam's tumble through the darkness felt like an eternity. There was no up nor down, left nor right. Just the ever expanding blackness. He was always in the Furnaces when he was not conscious. This place was void of anything what so ever. Sam was alone with his thoughts.

He questioned if this was what Malice experienced when Sam was in control? Malice was always capable of providing Sam with a place that had some basic laws to it like gravity. He had never given the monster that much credit. He never developed a place to keep him occupied. The only thing he ever gave Malice was a wall. In this way, Malice was a far more civil person than he was.

Perhaps Malice was so evil due to Sam's neglect of him. He had offered him no conversation. He gave him no comfort. The only thing Sam ever did for his demon was let him rot in the most heinous of prisons: emptiness. The relationship between the two was always an adversarial one. A constant battle for control over the outer shell was the norm between the two. When Sam finally built the wall up high enough, he left the monster behind it to wither and die. The only attention that was ever given was to the wall that imprisoned him.

Truly, Sam was the monster. He thought that by locking the problem up, it would go away. Nothing was further from the truth. Containing malice apparently gave him too much time to think. It made him very powerful and allowed him to learn about the inner workings of Sam's mind. Until now, Sam only worried about the thoughts in the forefront of his mind. He never concerned himself with the deeper workings.

Malice was always looking for a crack in the wall. Though Sam chose only to repair the cracks on this side of the wall, he could always feel Malice trying to escape and made no attempts to repair the wall from Malice's side. It was a mistake that he was currently paying the price for.

His mind continued to wander as he floated. Hoping and wishing for light. A beacon that he could focus on. His prayers were answered. In the distance, he could make out a faint glow. It was not the glow of a bright light or the tunnel so many had talked about in life after death experiences. The light was more like the warm glow of the fire in a very large cave; only illuminating whatever was near it.

The soft light acted as a beacon. It called to him. Drawing him into its warm embrace. Sam could not feel any ill will or deceitful intent coming from it, only security. As it pulled him closer, familiar things revealed themselves to him. The smell of rock and dirt mixed with burning wood. The wind as it passed over his ears and forced itself into his eyes causing them to water. The feeling of gravity with its vivacious pull toward the light. The feeling of pain as his body impacted with the ground. The taste and gritty feel of dust as it passed over his tongue and particles of it followed the air into his lungs. The ground he just crashed into was cool. This place was certainly not the Furnaces.

Not being one to meander around on the ground, Sam was quickly up to his feet. There was little definition in this place. The ground that Sam stood on was covered in loose dirt and small random stones. A quick turning of the head would reveal little else in sight except a man standing with his back towards Sam holding a torch. The light from the torch was harsh in his eyes, but Sam was able to make out a few details.

The man's silhouette revealed he was dressed in loose clothing and stood at Sam's height. He said nothing and moved even less. His statuesque manners left Sam wondering if he was merely a statue.

"What is this place?" Sam questioned.

The man said nothing. His silence was either in defiance of Sam's presence or he just simply had nothing to say. Sam beckoned to him once again.

"Who are you? Where am I?"

The figure remained silent. Instead of speaking, the shadowy figure began to walk away from Sam, taking the fire and the light away with him. Sam certainly didn't want to be left behind. He had enough of the darkness as well. With a few quick steps, he bridged the distance between himself and the man. Placing his hand on the figure's shoulder, Sam gave him a quick spin.

The appearance of the man's face was not what Sam expected to see. Black smoke and ash wisped upward from a skull that was partially covered by muscle and tissue. The figure screamed in pain and torment. It's torch erupted into a behemoth flame that illuminated the black sky revealing thousands of writhing bodies being ripped to shreds by Malice's black tar-like fluid. The horror of the sight was almost enough to make Sam puke. It was far more than he cared to see, but like a terrible accident, Sam could not take his eyes off the undulating mass of pain and suffering.

The flame died down, and the blackness returned. Sam was much happier not being able to see what was hidden in the darkness. The gruesome figure slowly turned around and began to walk away toward an unknown destination with a slow stagger.

The two men walked through the darkness for what appeared like an eternity to Sam. The distance was immeasurable. He refused to count his steps. He just walked. Step after grueling step. Spending the entire time in his head with his misery. All there was to focus on was the agonizing feeling of self-loathing. If there was a Hell, he was walking through it.

All was not lost, though. On the horizon, Sam was able to make out the faint appearance of a structure. From the distance he was at it was barely even visible. But as the two of them drew closer, it appeared the structure stretched in each direction beyond the horizon.

Where was he being led too? What was the place that this ghastly creature in front of him was taking him to? Was it the outer gates of Hell? Was this another trick of Malice's? All of his questions would obviously be answered in time. For now, he would only have his thoughts to worry about.

He would need to come to terms with himself. Julia was dead. Frank was dead. There was no way to change it unless these new godlike powers gave him the ability to bring people back to life. His remorse for the loss of the two most important people in his life was killing him at the moment. If he was ever given the chance to get back to the real world, he was going to need to get a grip on these powers. Get out of the city where there were so many innocent people.

His sulking and depressive state would have to wait. The megalithic structure was approaching faster than he expected. The closer Sam got, the more details he could make out though there were few to see. The walls of the massive construction were made of a black stone that seemed to glisten with moisture. They stretched in each direction and appeared to go on forever upward. There were two torches that whipped and flickered on either side of the entrance. The entire thing was devoid of any decoration. As the two of them reached the entrance, the silent and fearsome creature that Sam followed to this place stopped. Sam walked up beside him.

"I guess this is where I am supposed to be going, huh?" he said.

The creature just growled at him without moving.

"Don't worry. He doesn't like any of us. I do have to say he is not particularly fond of you, though." A voice spoke from the darkness.

Sam looked around in an attempt to pinpoint the location of the voice. He finally connected it to a figure that emerged from the black and introduced himself.

"I am Wei Jin. I am going to help you get out of this place," he said.

"What is this place? Who are you? And more importantly, what the hell is this thing?" Sam rattled off pointing at the thing that guided him here.

"This place is a plane of existence that you created in your mind when you ascended the first time. It is just adjacent to hell." Wei Jin explained. "I am your new teacher, by command of my Lord Almighty."

"You mean Ismael, right?" Sam queried.

"Yes. It is Ismael's will that I am here to help you learn. That thing is Death. He doesn't like you very much because you are keeping a lot of souls from him; yours included."

"Wait, what? Death? As in THE Death?" Sam questioned

"Yes. He is the being responsible for returning all living energy back into the universe. When someone dies, he cleanses that soul of its memories and recycles it back into the flow," Wei Jin answered. "There is one for every planet that harbors life in the universe."

"Uh-huh," Sam stated. Yesterday, he would have called bullshit on this guy. Today, he was willing to accept anything. "So why is he so pissed at me again?" he asked.

"You have not learned to release the souls that you have taken. Everyone that has died because of your direct action is still with you. You harbor their energy. Death cannot take them from you; you must release them."

"Let me make sure I get this right. I keep the souls of those I kill. What about normal people? What happens when they kill someone? Does the soul stay with them?" Sam was full of questions. His heightened intellect was in overdrive. He wanted to know about everything.

Wei Jin was patient and understanding in answering these questions. He knew that Sam changed into this form only hours ago, and the ascension process left him with a lot to learn.

"For the average mortal that takes another soul, both are released when the living one dies. A murderer will give his soul and the soul of the person he killed when he dies. Death does not have to wait long.

We are different. Death must wait until we breathe our last breath before he can claim the souls we take. That is why it is important that we learn to release those souls when we take them. Otherwise, it disrupts the flow. The universe will then manifest ways to correct that flow. Generally, to our downfall."

Wei Jin's words rang with a bit of truth in Sam's ears. He was inclined to believe what the asian was saying because he had no basis for comparison.

"You said this place is adjacent to Hell. What does that mean?" Sam asked as he cocked his head to the side. He had always heard of Heaven and Hell but never believed in them.

"Good question. Allow me to demonstrate." Wei Jin's hand began to glow a fiery bright yellow as he raised it above his head. The energy circulated and grew rapidly just before he released a massive burst into the sky. It exploded like a firework that did not burn out, illuminating the darkness and once again revealing the undulating mass of bodies being ripped to shreds.

"This is Hell. These souls are the ones that have died by you hand or by direct actions from you. They are trapped here until you can release them." Wei Jin explained with a bitter directness that struck a chord in Sam's heart. All of the people that he killed in the past few days were being ripped apart. Their deaths already weighed heavy on his heart, but to know that they were suffering beyond death because of his ignorance was more than he could bear.

"Oh God," Sam's voice cracked with the overpowering sound of remorse. The real consequences of his actions were hitting him like a Mack truck.

"Your Hell is a particularly nasty one. There is a lot of darkness in your heart Sam Rittenhouse. Most people that are damned to Hell simply float in the black abyss like you did when you got here. These souls are suffering immensely. I suspect it is because your Hell is governed by the creature you carry with you. I believe you call him Malice."

"Is he still alive? Is he killing more people?" Sam barked.

"No. I was able to render him unconscious. However, a man by the name of Cain took your body and left us only your head. You are currently being spun to prevent your resurrection."

"Spun?"

"Your body would need about a month to regenerate itself and bring about your next ascension. We cannot allow you to ascend again until you have Malice under control, and we have taught you to use your powers properly. I have placed the molecules below your neck into a perpetual spin. This prevents them from connecting, thus stopping the regeneration process. But I am not powerful enough to place you in complete suspension. You will eventually regenerate and ascend despite my sincerest efforts. The world is not prepared for Malice if he gains control at the point of ascension."

"Uuuuhhhhhhhh...shit. That's a lot to choke down. How long do we have?"

"Not long enough. You have been in suspension for three months. It took me this long to build a connection. I can keep you suspended for another three years if my calculations are correct."

"Three years. I am going to lose three years of my life?" Sam belted out in disbelief.

"You may live to be ten thousand years old Sam. Three years is a drop of water in an ocean. Honestly, it is not nearly enough time to train you. I spent sixty-three years teaching Ismael the martial arts. You have to learn more than that if you are to do the things my Lord Almighty expects of you."

Sam still had very little concept of what his power allowed him to do. If he was going to be here, he might as well learn. He was blown away by all the information that he just ingested. Death, Hell, being spun, releasing souls. Sam understood every bit of it. He was going to need to ask a lot of questions and pay close attention. Wei Jin was a lot more forthcoming than Michael was.

Sam took in a very deep breath and exhaled slowly. He looked Wei Jin directly in the eye and asked: "Where do we start?"

You start by entering this maze. I have created this place for you to learn. It is full of training opportunities. It is similar to the training ground I created for Ismael after his third ascension."

"This is a maze huh? What is in there?" asked Sam.

"We shall see. I hope that you have filled it with many things. However, only time will tell."

"It's like *Star Wars* and *The Matrix* mixed with a bit of Labyrinth. I dig it."

Sam took in another deep breath and rubbed his hands together in an attempt to psych himself up. He held his head high and threw his shoulders back and confidently walked into the maze.

Thank you for reading my story. This book is the first in a series. I write a lot of fiction. If you enjoyed this fiction, please feel free to find me online. This series of books has its own website.

12BlackenedPetals.com

I also write a blog. It's a pretty funny site. All of the posts are written from the viewpoint of a cynical super villain turned hero. If you go to this site and sign up for the email list, I will inform you of new posts, updates on the novel I am writing at the time, and even some short stories and bonus content you can't get anywhere else.

BriansDailyGrind.com